Watch Out for the Big Girls 2

Watch Out for the Big Girls 2

J. M. Benjamin

URBAN BOOKS

www.urbanbooks.net

Urban Books, LLC
97 N18th Street
Wyandanch, NY 11798

Watch Out for the Big Girls 2

ISBN 13: 978-1-62286-725-7
ISBN 10: 1-62286-725-4

First Trade Paperback Printing December 2016
Printed in the United States of America

10 9 8 7 6 5 4 3 2 1

Distributed by Kensington Publishing Corp.
Submit orders to:
Customer Service
400 Hahn Road
Westminster, MD 21157-4627
Phone: 1-800-733-3000
Fax: 1-800-659-2436

Dedicated to the Bold & Beautiful

Prologue

The Birth of Queen Fem and the "G" Files
1989

Twenty-five-year-old Carlita Banks sat in front of her bedroom mirror teary-eyed, stroking her shoulder-length dark, wavy hair after she had applied a little eyeliner and lip gloss to her natural beauty. It was unlike the heavy makeup she once wore. Just a year ago, she stood in front of a rest stop's filthy bathroom mirror somewhere outside of Los Angeles, California, resembling a sad clown's face with tear-filled eyes and runny makeup, looking a hot mess. She found herself there after a well-known and powerful figure in the political world had forced himself on her. That was during a charity event she had managed to sneak into in an attempt to work the crowd. She trembled at the thought of it as her mind drifted back in time. After the rape, his threat to have her killed if he ever saw her face again was enough for her to flee the city of L.A. and return to her hometown.

Now, here it was; her tears of sorrow were replaced with tears of joy. She never thought what she had felt was possible. A huge grin appeared across Carlita's face at the thought. She would have never imagined in a million years that one person could ever make her feel so happy and alive, especially after all she had been through. But the man whose car she reluctantly got into that same day a year ago as she stood on the side of the road with her thumb out proved her wrong.

Carlita turned and checked the time on her wall clock. It read 10:35. Within the year she had known him, she had learned that he was a stickler about time. It was his pet peeve. She knew she had to be dressed and ready to go in the next fifty-five minutes. She sprayed herself with his favorite perfume and then stood and made her way over toward her bed. She laid her eggshell white evening gown out. Neatly, she then placed on the diamond-studded key-shaped medallion dangling from a necklace that had arrived earlier. She smiled as the words on the note illuminated in her mind for the umpteenth time: *"This is the key to my heart; you've earned it. I want you looking special for when I ask you something special later this evening."* Butterflies filled her stomach and her heart skipped a beat each time she replayed the words in her head.

Forty minutes later, Carlita stood in front of her living room's wall mirror looking like a million bucks. She ran her hands down the sides of her protruding hips and her midriff as if she were smoothing out some last-minute wrinkles in her dress. The new ten pounds she had added to her once 135-pound frame went in all the right places. She stood breathtaking at five feet six. The six-inch sling-back stilettos she wore boosted her natural fun-size height of five feet. They also enhanced the arch in her back. The tops of her breasts fluffed up perfectly in her dress. It gave her the look of a black stallion. The diamonds in her medallion sparkled in the mirror as it rested just above Carlita's cleavage.

The phrase "one person's trash is another's treasure" came to her mind. At that moment, Carlita felt like a real-life Cinderella because twelve months ago she had nothing. She was living a dangerous lifestyle out of cheap motels, working the casinos and clubs from California to Las Vegas for scores; and she allowed men to use and abuse her for money to survive. Now, she was in love with a powerful man who made her feel safe and gave her everything her heart desired. She couldn't see herself wanting any other man in her life, or another man touching her ever again.

The sound of his car's engine outside her door caused Carlita's heart to skip a beat. It was a sound she had never really gotten used to, being in her line of work. But it made her reflect on the first time the sound of one of his many vehicles had made her react that way. She had made countless poor choices and decisions in her young life. But that day, she was glad she had made the one she had. She'd never forget the day she climbed into the silver Mercedes-Benz 560. She always believed it was a sign from God for her to get out of L.A. as she rode in the luxury car. It couldn't haven't been planned any better when the owner of the Mercedes said his final destination was her intended one: Las Vegas, Nevada.

Once again, the words from the note invaded her young mind. She already had a strong guess as to what that special question he wanted to ask her would be. Carlita snatched up her clutch and opened the front door to the townhouse he had put her in two weeks after he'd convinced her to stay with him once they arrived in Vegas. She nearly fainted at the sight of him. He stood next to his black Maserati with the passenger door wide open, waiting for her. She smiled inside at how debonair he looked in his all-black tuxedo, white shirt, and black bowtie. His smooth midnight complexion matched his suit, and his milk white smile matched his shirt. He was the most handsome man Carlita had ever laid eyes on. His deep, dark waves would make anyone seasick and his razor-sharp shape up looked as if it would draw blood from anybody who touched it. She could smell his Gucci cologne from her doorstep. It wasn't loud but, rather, alluring.

His baritone voice broke Carlita out of her trance. "Your chariot awaits, madam." He bowed his head and extended his hand in her direction.

Carlita smiled at his gesture. "Thank you, sir." She returned his bow.

Moments later, Carlita was safely in the car, relaxing to the sound of Marvin Gaye as they headed to their intended destination.

"Good evening, ma'am," the valet announced as he helped Carlita out of the sports car.

Carlita noticed that a variety of Rolls-Royces, Porsches, Lamborghinis, and limousines were in front of, alongside, and behind her lover's Maserati as they exited the vehicle. Between that and the size and style of the home, she knew there were some very important people in attendance. He had taken her out and wined and dined her at some extravagant places in the past and she noticed the love and respect he had received from faces she had only seen on television or read about in the newspaper, but this was different. In the entire year they had known each other, she had never asked him what he did for a living and he had never volunteered, but she knew he had power and was connected both legally and in the underworld.

Carlita held on to his arm as he escorted her to the front entrance. He handed the doorman two invitations and guided her inside the plush mansion. For a second, a sense of nervousness swept through Carlita's body. The last time she was in that type of setting a man had forced himself on her. She tightened her grip around her lover's arm.

He looked down at her. "What's wrong, love?" he asked.

She looked up into his deep brown eyes and felt safe all over again. She had never told him what had happened to her or what she had been through and he had never

pressured her to. She also never told him why she had
stayed when he had asked. It was those very same eyes
that offered her safety now that convinced her to stay
back then.

"Nothing." She smiled. "Felt a little lightheaded for a
second, but I'm fine."

He kissed her on the forehead. "Well, hopefully that
makes you feel better." He matched her smile.

Just then a heavyset, older white gentleman with a
model-type beauty who looked to be half his age stopped
in front of them. "This must be Mrs. Steele," the man
announced.

Carlita thought the man looked familiar. Her lover
smiled proudly. "Yes, it is," he replied. "And this must
be—"

Before he could finish his sentence the heavyset man
drowned his words out with laughter. "I know I don't
have to tell you that you have a unique man on your
hands, Mrs. Steele. Pleasure meeting you. You two enjoy
the rest of your evening. Lewis, I'll be in touch." The
heavyset man ended abruptly and strolled off without
introducing the woman who accompanied him.

Carlita noticed her lover shaking his head. He let out a
light chuckle.

"Honey, who was that and what was all that about?"
she asked.

"That was Councilman Dickhead and that was about
nothing. Let's just enjoy ourselves," he suggested.

The campaign commercial she had seen countless
times of the councilman immediately appeared in
Carlita's mind. The slogan *I'm here to serve you* rang
out in Carlita's head, as an image of the councilman's
face appeared in her mind.

Lewis Steele snatched up two flutes of champagne
from one of the servers passing by and handed one to

Carlita. "To us!" He tapped his flute to Carlita's and made a toast.

"To us!" Carlita repeated as she gazed into his eyes. She raised the glass of champagne to her lips and tossed it back until her flute was empty.

Lewis grinned and tossed his back like a shot of bourbon. He took her flute and put them both on a passing waiter's tray. He then turned back toward Carlita and dropped his head. He gave her a juicy but quick kiss on the lips, before arching his arm. "Shall we?" He smiled with his eyes.

"We shall." Carlita matched his smiling eyes.

For the next two hours, Lewis Steele cordially and casually mixed and mingled with the crowd, each time introducing Carlita as Mrs. Steele. After every small talk session, Lewis would give Carlita a brief history on the politician or law official she'd just met. Each story would end with the individual being crooked. At first, Carlita wondered how Lewis could know so much about so many people, but after her third glass of bubbly she couldn't care less about the who, what, when, where, and why about anything.

The evening had calmed down and people poured out of the luxury home and spilled outside. By now, Carlita was somewhat tipsy from the six glasses of expensive bubbly she had managed to consume throughout the course of the evening. Lewis guided her inside of his car then closed the passenger door. Carlita reclined her seat and closed her eyes. Her dress was now hiked up, and exposed her thick legs.

Lewis stretched his hand and caressed her inner thigh. "Bae, don't fall asleep. The night isn't over yet," Lewis told her.

"Uh-huh," she moaned. She could barely keep her eyes open. The thousand-dollar-a-bottle champagne had been well spent and served its purpose when it came to Carlita's share.

Lewis laughed to himself and smiled. He slithered his hand farther up Carlita's dress as Al Green filled the car with his melodic voice. He could feel the heat between her legs as he parted them with his two fingers. Lewis slid her panties to the side and began fondling Carlita. She spread her legs wider and pushed his hand deeper under her dress. Lewis could feel her wetness. His dick stiffened. Carlita slowly gyrated her sex to match Lewis's fingers fondling her. Lewis massaged Carlita's clit vigorously. Carlita could feel her juices oozing down her inner thigh and through Lewis's fingers. Her body quivered. She removed Lewis's hand from between her legs and reached over into his lap. Lewis glanced over at her, only to see the devilish grin plastered across her face.

Carlita leaned over and began to unfasten her lover's belt. Within mere seconds, she had his rock-hard dick out of his briefs and in her mouth. Carlita could feel the horsepower of the car as Lewis accelerated. The sudden speed turned her on. She attacked Lewis's dick with her mouth. She licked alongside his pulsating veins then took him back into her mouth and deep throated him. Lewis placed his hand on the back of her head and guided her as she bobbed up and down on him while he navigated the Maserati with his other hand.

"Yes, baby," he cooed. "Right there." The impact of the hit broke his concentration and cut his words short.

"What the hell?" Lewis boomed. He quickly pulled his hand from the top of Carlita's head and gripped the steering wheel just in time to gain control of the car and avoid crashing.

Carlita had now risen up and was fully alert. "Lew, what's going on?" she cried.

Lewis peered into his rearview. His eyes widened as the headlights of the car behind them rapidly approached. Before he could answer Carlita, the back of his Maserati was rammed for a second time. This time the impact was more forceful than the first. The hit caused Lewis to spin out of control. Within seconds, the sports car was skidding down the road.

The last thing Carlita remembered before blacking out was staring into Lewis Steele's deep brown eyes. She looked for that safety he had provided her for the past year of her life.

The sound of a gunshot was what caused Carlita to jump out of her unconscious state, but the sound of yelling and laughter was what caused her to open her eyes. Once she regained her vision, the first thing she saw was a young white male hovering over her. His words alarmed her to the imminent danger she was in.

"His bitch is woke," the young white male chimed.

"Good. Bring her black ass over here," one of the five men surrounding Lewis Steele commanded.

"Come here." The young white male roughly grabbed a fistful of Carlita's hair. She screamed out in agony as he dragged her over to where Lewis lay.

She immediately burst into tears at the sight of her lover. She noticed one of the men standing over Lewis's body, zipping up his pants. Lewis was covered in his own blood. Both of his eyes were nearly shut and swollen. His mouth leaked of blood and his lips were busted. Blood oozed from the top of his head where an open gash existed. The stench of strong urine caused Carlita to gag. She nearly vomited.

"Why are you doing this?" Carlita yelled. "What do you want from us?"

Her words caused more laughter among the men. "Aw, she really doesn't know," one of the men mocked.

"I bet she doesn't know about this, either," another one of the men chimed in.

Carlita looked up and over at the man. She noticed the red velvet ring box he held in his hand. More tears spilled out of her eyes. She knew the red velvet box was the reason behind the special question Lewis intended to ask her.

"Give me that!" Carlita reached out and tried to grab the box from the man's hand. Instead of accomplishing what she set out to do, she was compensated with a backhand across the face. The blow sent her tumbling. She landed on her lover.

"You stupid bitch," the man spat. He moved in to deliver another blow but was stopped in his tracks.

"That's enough," another man calmly stated. "Let's just see if she knows anything," he continued.

The other men nodded in agreement. The man then kneeled down in front of Carlita. He began stroking her hair and the side of her face. Carlita cringed from his touch.

"Now listen carefully, sweetheart. You can save yourself and your soon-to-be fiancé if you just do us this little favor and tell us what we need to know. Understand?"

Carlita nodded.

"Good girl." He smiled. "Now, Lewis here has some very important information that could do a lot of people some harm if it falls into the wrong hands. Before that happens we'd like it back. The problem is Lewis refuses to tell us where we can find this information. And since we know he doesn't have a lot of friends and doesn't really trust anyone, we figured you'd be the only person who would know and he would tell in case something like this ever happened."

Carlita listened attentively. It all made sense to her now, how Lewis knew all he did about important and powerful people. Her mind was racing a hundred miles a minute. She couldn't believe Lewis refused to give up what he had to save himself and her. She felt betrayed and abandoned. There was no doubt in her mind that she was going to die where she lay because she simply could not give the man the answer he was looking for.

She stared at the man kneeling in front of her for the first time. She recognized him from the party they had just left. She did a quick scan and realized she recognized all of the men from the party. The only difference was at the party they wore police uniforms, versus the plain clothes they wore now.

Carlita cleared her throat. "Honestly," she started out with, "I don't know anything."

"Man, fuck this!" one of the men yelled. "We wasted enough time already. The fuckin' nigger didn't tell us shit and now his bitch is playing stupid too. If we kill both their asses they can't use the information anyway." His words riled up the other men.

"I'm with Johnny on this one, Luke," one of the other men joined in.

The remaining men nodded in agreement as well.

"Everybody just chill the fuck out," the man known as Luke ordered in his calm tone. "Honey, are you sure you don't know anything about a black book of names, a ledger, anything?"

"I swear to you, I don't know nothing about nothing," she assured him.

The man known as Luke rose up. "That's too bad." He frowned and then turned his back on her.

"Kill 'em," he nonchalantly stated.

The man known as Johnny wasted no time. He raised his weapon and pointed it at Carlita. Her eyes widened with fear. The shot to the head knocked her backward. She felt the additional two shots rip into her body just before darkness came.

The sound of her doorbell caused Carlita's eyes to shoot open. "Just a minute," she yelled as she rose out of the bed. She slipped into her slippers. A sharp pain jolted in her lower back. She took a deep breath, blew it out, and shook the pain off. Since being released from the hospital six days ago it had been a struggle for her. She was lucky to be alive. Due to the shot she took to the head, she still had no recollection of what happened to her or how she ended up in the hospital. The doctor told her that she was suffering from selective amnesia and, with time, some if not all of her memory would be restored.

"Who is it?" Carlita asked as she cautiously made her way to the door. Ever since she had been home she had been on edge. The fact that she couldn't remember how she had gotten shot both puzzled and frightened her.

Although she heard who was at the door, she still looked through the peephole. She saw a young brown-skinned male dressed in a UPS shorts set.

"How may I help you?" she asked.

"Delivery for a Ms. Carlita Banks," the UPS worker announced.

Hearing her name, Carlita relaxed and opened the door.

She was greeted with a smile. "Are you Ms. Banks?"

Carlita nodded.

"Please sign here."

Carlita took the plastic pen and signed the keypad the UPS worker presented her.

"Thank you. Have a nice day." The UPS worker handed Carlita an envelope then scurried off.

Carlita closed the door. She stared at the return address. The name L. STEELE was on the envelope. The name didn't ring a bell to her.

"L. Steele," she said aloud. "L. Steele," she closed her eyes and repeated. An image appeared in her head. She did not recognize the handsome man she saw. Carlita tore open the envelope. The first sentences of the letter jumped out at her:

Hello, my queen. If you're reading this then the worst has happened.

Carlita could feel her heart rate increasing. She continued reading the letter.

I was hoping it wouldn't come to this, but I knew there was always a possibility. That's why I made provisions for you in case of an emergency, to secure your safety. I pray you still have the key to my heart. That key is also the key to your safety and the key to avenging me.

Go to the address below and use that key to enter from the back. This map will lead you to where you need to be. Once you are inside and you reach your destination, your birth date will be the next key to unlock the truth. There you will find what you need, from funds to information, in order to survive.

When you locate and learn what you need to know, move as far away as you can from Las Vegas, but make them all pay. Use both the money and the information wisely and productively. I trust and believe that you will. If this letter reaches you before our special night then that means I never got the honor and pleasure of making you my wife. But just know, in my mind, you already were. I couldn't see myself with any other woman but you, and I hope you felt the same way about me.

The statement caused Carlita's heart to flutter. Images of her and the handsome man she envisioned moments ago flashed through her mind. In each image, she bore a smile and beamed with joy. She watched as the footage of the man helping her into the sports car played in her head. The scene flashed from the car to the inside of a luxurious mansion. Little by little the scenes started to become familiar to Carlita.

Her eyes widened as the image appeared of her performing oral sex on the man. If she didn't know before, she knew now that the man was someone special to her. Her body jumped at the sudden scene of the car spinning out of control. That image quickly turned into the scene of her on her knees while a group of white men hovered over the man. The sight of the ring box in the man's hand triggered something in Carlita's mind and heart. Tears spilled out of her eyes and onto her face as the white man's words pierced her heart. The explosion of the gun pointed at her head brought Carlita back to the present. What was once a blur was now clear. She knew exactly who the man in the images was and what he meant to her. Carlita's tears increased as she relived the whole ordeal.

"Lewis!" she cried out. She fell to the floor and buried her face in the palm of her hands. For the next hour, Carlita bawled her eyes out nonstop. Once she was done, she dried her eyes and pulled herself back together. Carlita reread the letter from Lewis Steele. She took a moment to gather her thoughts then rose and made her way to her bedroom. As she dressed, all she could think about was where the key that dangled from her necklace would lead her to.

Later That Evening

As instructed, Carlita nervously entered through the back of the Rancho Circle home she had managed to locate. She was familiar with that particular part of the city only by name. It didn't surprise her that her deceased lover owned a home in the million-dollar, small-community area. Carlita took one last look around. Convinced she had gone unnoticed, Carlita entered and closed the door to the mysterious house behind her.

She used what little light her cell phone provided her to guide her through what appeared to be an enormous, empty house. Confusion appeared on Carlita's face. There were absolutely no furnishings in sight, nor was there anything on the walls to indicate that the home had been lived in. Carlita shined her phone light on the map she possessed in her hand. Her eyes went from the map to what was in front of her as she made her way to the staircase the piece of paper led her to. Once up the steps, she turned to the right as instructed and opened the first door she came in contact with.

Her legs nearly collapsed and she nearly fainted from the sweet, familiar smell she had grown to love. His fragrance illuminated the spacious room as if he were standing in it at that very moment. The presence of Lewis Steele was in what she believed to be her ex-lover's fully equipped office. The room had his name written all over it: stylish, professional, and neatly organized. Carlita studied the map for a second. She then made her way to the wooden mahogany-colored desk. She sat in the leather swivel chair. Her heart fluttered at the sight of the framed picture of the two of them in Hawaii. She couldn't bear to look at the photo, so she leaned in and laid it face down on the desk. Carlita then reached under the desk and ran her hand along the bottom part of the counter. Within seconds, the left side wall began to slide open.

Carlita's eyes widened. She rose up and headed over toward the sliding wall, which had now revealed a metal door. Carlita noticed the door had a keypad that required numbers. She slowly punched in the number 0225. She took a step back as the metal door slid open. She shined her phone in front of her. It lit up the staircase that led downward. Carlita took a deep breath. Then she placed her hand on the right side of the wall and took the steps to her final destination. As she reached the bottom of the steps her hand brushed past a switch. Instinctively, Carlita hit the switch and the basement-level room lit up like the Christmas tree in New York City at Rockefeller Center.

Carlita couldn't believe her eyes. The room looked like a scene straight out of a James Bond movie. It was full of electronics, from monitor screens and VCR players to switchboards and video cameras. The walls were lined with file cabinets. What stood out about them most was the fact that they were labeled with titles rather than alphabetized.

Carlita was instantly drawn to the file cabinet titled LAW ENFORCEMENT. She walked over toward the cabinet and opened it. Inside, each section was classified by a specific name. Carlita thumbed through the sections. She randomly picked one of the folders, titled UNDERAGE ACTIVITY, which contained a file and a video tape.

Moments later, Carlita was sitting in front of the huge monitor screen with a look of disgust plastered across her face, fast-forwarding through the disturbing footage. Her blood boiled as she watched four uniformed Caucasian police officers participate in a sexual orgy with two females who appeared to be well under the legal age. In mid-view, she paused the tape and leaned in closer to the screen. Her eyes grew cold at the sight of the familiar face. The image of the man urinating on her ex-lover appeared in her mind as she made the connection. In an instant, it all became clear to Carlita. For the next few hours, she went through many of what seemed to be hundreds of files.

That night, Carlita Banks died and a new woman was born. By the time she left the house, she knew what she had to do and how it had to be done.

One Month Later

Councilman John Busch opened the front door of his mini-mansion in his bathrobe. His stomach protruded as he stood in his doorway the way he did every morning, shirtless, in Fruit of the Loom underwear, with a Cuban cigar dangling from his mouth. He removed the cigar from his mouth, stretched, and took in the early morning Las Vegas air. He then kneeled down and retrieved the Sunday newspaper. A headline almost caused him to tumble over. He rose and peered from left to right. He noticed a manila envelope lying on his front step. It was addressed to him. Beads of sweat began to form on his forehead. *No, it can't be,* he thought as he went inside and slammed his front door behind him. He plopped down onto his living room sofa and reread the top headline of the newspaper: OFFICERS FOUND DEAD IN CONNECTION WITH UNDERAGE TEENS.

Rather than read the article, Councilman Busch felt the content of the package before tearing it open. Inside were two videos. They each possessed a note stating PLAY ME, along with a letter inside. John Busch wasted no time popping in the first VHS tape. As he had expected, the first tape he put in was a copy of his constituents engrossed in illegal sexual activities with minors. He immediately ejected it, put the second tape in, and pushed play on his remote. He smacked his forehead hard with the palm of his hand and shook his head at the footage.

Councilman John Busch's heart nearly stopped as the sight of him and his young male lover appeared across his television screen. He knew there was only one person who was in possession of this footage besides himself and he was under the impression that person was dead. Judging by the headlines of Sunday's paper and the footage he had just moments ago viewed, Councilman John Busch was not so sure that was the case. He fought to pull out the letter he had received in the envelope. The letter was comprised of words clipped out of magazines. *To cover their tracks, of course,* thought Councilman Busch. As soon as he started reading the letter, John Busch turned beet red.

Hello, you cock sucker! It seems your fetish for little boys has finally caught up to you. I'm sure you thought it was over. But this is only the beginning. Had I no use for you, you would already be dead, like your friends. You can try your luck and go to the police with this, but if you know what's best you'll side against it. The footage you received is stored away in a computer file along with hundreds of others. As long as you do what you are told, when you are told, that's where it will remain.

If you choose to retaliate or show resistance in any kind of way, shape, form, or fashion, you will be killed just as those who rebelled. But only after you've been stripped of everything and every person you love or even cared about. And on top of all that, the footage will be played at your funeral. Copies will be handed out to everyone throughout the entire state of Nevada connected or associated with you. Your legacy will be tarnished and reduced to dirt. And all you would be known for is being an ex-politician who was a closet queen, and lost his life due to politics because he fucked with the wrong person and got fucked. I will be in touch!

Yours Truly,

Queen of the Double Gs

"Son of a bitch!" John Busch cursed aloud. He balled up the letter and tossed it at the television. A million thoughts raced through his mind.

"Honey, is everything okay?"

Councilman Busch's train of thought was broken by the sound of his wife's voice as she entered the living room. With record-breaking speed, Councilman John Busch managed to shut off the VCR tape that was still showing on his television.

"Everything's fine, my dear. Go back to bed."

Chapter 1

Starrshma Fields sat in the freezing cold cell, using nothing but her most sinister thoughts to keep her warm. She pulled her knees into her chest and wrapped her arms around them and locked her fingers. She used the silence to her advantage. She thought about the chain of events that led up to her sitting in the cold and desolate cell. She thought about how things began taking a turn for the worse after the day she had received the first anonymous call about an informant being planted in their organization.

She played the tape back in her mind. All the facial expressions and reactions among each Double G when she presented the disturbing phone call to them, from the newest member down to her most trusted, illuminated in her mind. When she'd first received the call from the anonymous caller informing her that she had snitch in the organization she didn't want to believe it. As she sat in the federal holding cell, she was convinced that the anonymous caller was telling the truth for whatever reason.

Her thoughts switched to the agents tailing her and her last meeting with Queen Fem. She didn't want to believe that her mentor had a hand in the recent events that had been transpiring; but lately they had been butting heads more than ever. She knew better than anybody just how ruthless and vindictive Queen Fem could be. After all, she was her protégé.

Queen Fem had practically raised her and taught her everything she knew. One of the most valuable lessons Queen Fem had expressed to her was that, in her line of work, no one was exempt from being a suspect when things got thick. But Starr also knew Queen Fem loved her as if she had given birth to her, despite their recent head-butting.

A million thoughts ran through Starrshma Fields's mind, but there were only a few of them she intended to look into once she made it out of the holding cell. After speaking to Diamond, she was sure they didn't have anything on her. But if they did she knew it was just a matter of time before whatever it was slipped through their fingers.

Starr's train of thought was broken by the echoing sound of hard-bottom shoes walking down the corridor while orders were being shouted and answers to questions were being demanded. The voices grew louder and closer, until Agent Reddick's red face appeared in front of Starr's cell door.

"You heartless bitch! You're going to fry in hell for what you did!" Agent Reddick wasted no time cutting into Starr. "I can't prove it now, but you best believe you will stand accountable for the deaths of those three agents and all the others I'm sure you had a hand in, Ms. Fields."

Starr stared at him stone-faced as he ranted and raved. All the other agents stood in the background with their arms folded and just listened.

"Yeah, go ahead, act like a tough guy. You don't freaking scare me. You think having little children killed makes you big and bad!" It was more of a rhetorical statement than a question.

Starr rolled her eyes and dismissed Agent Reddick.

"Don't you walk away from me when I'm fucking talking to you, you worthless piece of shit!"

His words slammed into Starr's back, causing a rise out of her. She immediately spun around and, in the blink of an eye, she was face to face with Agent Reddick. The only things that stood between them were metal bars, air, and opportunity.

Her sudden reaction caught Agent Reddick by surprise. It was as if he had become frozen in time when she grabbed a hold of his wrist. He was not expecting her to respond, let alone take action.

"Listen here, pig." Starr wasted no time checking him. Her tone was low but strong. "That was the last time you disrespect me. If there's a next time, it's going to cost you." Starr ended with a sinister smile.

Her words only heightened Agent Reddick's anger, but he was far from a dummy. The look in her eyes told him she meant what she had said to him. He could feel the pressure Starr was applying to his wrist. He snatched his arm away from Starr's grip. "Don't you ever fucking touch me again!" he boomed. "And don't you fucking threaten me, either!"

Starr just stood there grilling the agent. The other agents all looked at one another with confused looks plastered on their faces. Agent Reddick's jaws tightened as he matched Starr's stare. Although he would never openly admit it, Starr's threat had managed to penetrate his thoughts. He couldn't help but think about the wife and son he had at home. His thoughts were interrupted by the sultry voice behind him.

"I said, is there a problem here, gentlemen?" Diamond calmly repeated with hands on her hips.

When Agent Reddick turned around, he saw Starr's attorney, who also happened to be a member of the Double Gs, standing alongside his superior officer.

"What the hell is this?" Agent Reddick directed his words to his boss.

"We gotta let Ms. Fields go," Agent Reddick's supervisor announced. He held up the piece of paper he was holding in his left hand. "Orders from the attorney general's office."

Murmurs and disapproving grunts could be heard by the other agents.

"Are you fucking kidding me?" Agent Reddick spat in disgust. "Just like that, she walks?" His eyes shifted back and forth from Diamond to his supervisor.

All his supervisor could do was grimace. Seconds later, the cell door was opened and Starrshma Fields casually stepped out. Her eyes and Agent Reddick's locked for a second time.

"I'll be seeing you. Real soon!" Agent Reddick chimed.

Starr let out a light chuckle. "See you when you get there," she returned. "Gentlemen." She turned her attention to the agents who lined the wall. And then, just like that, she and Diamond strolled out of the Clark County federal holding facility.

Chapter 2

2014

"Fuuuuuuuuck!"Officer Douglass yelled hysterically. He pounded his fist against his head as he paced the cell. Tears spilled out of his eyes. "Somebody help!" he cried.

The only response he'd gotten was from his echo.

His mind was racing a million miles a minute. He could still hear the screams and cries of his wife and daughter. The shots still rang in his ears. He felt dizzy and faint. He knew it was his own fault. He knew the risk of coming forward. He had seen what they had done to others who had crossed them. He regretted the day he had encountered one of the Double Gs. Rather, the day his partner had.

He cursed the late Officer Blake for putting him in the predicament and position he was now faced with. Because of Officer Blake's crooked ways and craving for plus-sized black prostitutes, and the fact that Douglass had his partner's back once upon a time, the Double Gs were able to corrupt him. Now, since blowing the whistle on everything, his family was dead.

Unable to take it any longer, Officer Douglass broke into a violent rage. He began banging on the walls, kicking the sink, and doing whatever else he thought would get someone's attention. He needed to know whether what he heard over the phone was true or just a mere scare tactic. He prayed that they were just trying to scare him, to show him that they could get to him and his family.

The calmness of the woman's voice through the phone had alarmed him. He knew, firsthand, about the kind of vindictive women he was dealing with, but he never figured they would go this far. *My wife? My daughter? No. This has to be a warning. Pretty soon, Loretta and Cameron will come visit me with a message, pleading for me to change my mind about double-crossing those Double Gs,* he reasoned with himself.

Officer Douglass felt defeated. He cursed himself for not securing his wife and daughter before he made his decision to come clean. He had underestimated the lengths the organization he was trying to contribute to taking down would go and he knew better. *Why would my family be exempt from their wrath when they're known for making people pay for crossing them?* he questioned himself. He knew he would have to accept whatever lawful punishment he was subjected to in exchange for the safety of his family. Thinking about watching his daughter Cameron grow up from behind a prison wall put a bad taste in his mouth. But at least she would be safe, he concluded.

His thoughts were broken by the sound of the guard coming through the door. The person trailing the guard caused his heart to drop to the pit of his stomach He rushed to the cell bars. "No!" Officer Douglass clenched the metal bars and chimed.

"I'm sorry, my son." The chaplain leaned in toward Officer Douglass with a rosary's beaded cross hanging out of the middle of the Bible, and he rested his right hand on top of his through the cell bars.

"Noooooo!" Officer Douglass snatched his hand away. He dropped to his knees and buried his face in his hands. His cries shook the walls and could be heard throughout the entire building.

Chapter 3

It was an emotional and on-edge day for the Bureau. First the funeral, then the unexpected occurrence with Agent McCarthy's daughter. He still couldn't believe the Double Gs had managed to take out a few of his colleagues and not have any ties or links to the murders. Had it not been for his daughter's illness he would still be leading the case. But his pride and joy being in the hospital with all sorts of tubes in her body had him an emotional wreck. It was impossible for him to focus on taking down the Double Gs when his baby girl needed him by her side. Once upon a time he wanted nothing more than to be the one responsible for disbanding the all-female organized crime gang, but his job was the furthest thing from his mind. Which was why he was not too enthused about receiving the call about a bank robbery.

Agent Reddick was all too ready to call it a day and go rest his mind. When he was informed he had to fill in for McCarthy on the bank job he was not too thrilled. The only reason he didn't argue with his supervisor and try to get out of it was because he was told that the bank job was in connection with the Double Gs. They had all been working around the clock to take down the organization and he didn't want to pass up an opportunity to contribute to that.

The words Agent Mobley had spoken at the funeral service were still resonating in his mind. *They were one of us and it could have been any one of us.* The deaths of the three agents had really hit home. If they didn't believe before, they were all believers now. The Double Gs were dangerous and had to be stopped.

He was all too familiar with how hard and diligently Agent McCarthy had been working on the Double Gs case. He respected him for his work that had awakened the agency to the Double Gs. He grimaced at the fact that he was guilty of indulging in conversations with other agents humorously at Agent McCarthy's expense. He was among those who believed Agent McCarthy was a washed-up, delusional agent. But Agent Reddick now knew that was not the case, as he stormed through the bank's revolving doors and headed straight behind the teller counter. He removed his sunglasses and stuck them into his windbreaker's inside pocket before kneeling down over the corpse and pulling the sheet back. He immediately noticed the victim had been shot execution style.

"There was something I believe was purposely left behind," another agent informed him.

"What?" Agent Reddick asked.

The agent handed Agent Reddick the paper that was left behind. He slowly unfolded it and read it all with one glance. He was all too familiar with the content. There were several of them in evidence already. It was the signature card of the Double Gs and anyone associated with them. Judging by the particular card, Agent Reddick was almost positive the bank job and hit was the work of the Spalding brothers. *Maybe they are just like the rest of them. Puppets. Maybe they turned the money over to those gotdamn she-devils,* Agent Reddick hypothesized.

"It all makes sense now," Agent Reddick concluded.

"What's that, sir?" the agent wanted to know.

"It explains what's been rattling my brain since the call came through," he began. "I mean, it didn't make sense to me at first. The Double Gs have more money than they know what to do with, I'm sure. So, why would they have their hands in robbing a bank?"

As he analyzed the scenario something else popped in Agent Reddick's head. He pulled out his cell phone. "This is Agent Reddick," he spoke into his phone. "I need the names of all members associated with the Double Gs organization who have been picked up or questioned recently," he instructed. "And see if any of them had any connections with any banks." Agent Reddick pulled his phone away from his ear while he waited for the information he had just requested.

"What's the victim's name?" he asked the agent.

The agent looked down at his notepad. "Uh, Pearson. Careese Pearson."

The name meant nothing to Agent Reddick.

Three minutes later, as the agent ran down the names and occupations of the Double Gs they had detained, questioned, or arrested, one name stood out above all and connected the dots for Agent Reddick.

"Thanks."Agent Reddick hung up his cell phone and turned his attention to the agent. "This wasn't just a bank robbery. It was a hit," he informed the agent.

"How do you know that, sir?"

"Because Careese Pearson was a Double G. Something we should have already made the connection to."

Chapter 4

The getaway was clean and easy but the ride was a quiet and an uncomfortable one. Every so often Felicia would cut her eyes over at Monica, who sat in the passenger seat in silence and on edge. She had every reason to be. The text message from the anonymous number had her all the way on point. The words *"Don't trust nobody!"* still played in her head. Although the text didn't offer anything more, it was enough to let Monica know she may possibly be in danger.

The way Felicia had looked at her, after receiving a message herself, had Monica on guard. The occasional glances over at her, and Felicia's silence throughout their ride, made her feel that danger may be closer than she realized. Monica's mind was racing a hundred miles a minute. She knew she was way in over her head and had reached the point of no return, but she knew she had been careful in her movements. She had followed orders and instructions to a T from day one and she wondered what could have fueled the text. She had no clue where Felicia was headed, but it was killing her not knowing what was going on. Monica turned to Felicia and decided to test the waters and feel her out.

"Is everything okay?" she asked.

Felicia peered over at her and flashed a half smile. There was a slight pause before she replied, "Everything's cool." Felicia's reply was short and flat, hard for Monica to read.

Monica matched her smile. "Good," was her response. Felicia gave her a thumbs-up and drew her attention back to the road. Her reaction only heightened the tension Monica was feeling.

Moments later, Felicia navigated her SUV onto a side road. The first thing Monica noticed was the open dirt field. There was nothing and no one else in sight other than a Mercedes-Benz. Monica's senses were on high alert. She questioned who the car belonged to. *Is this a trap?* she wondered. She was tempted to reach for her weapon tucked at her lower back, but sided against it out of fear of Felicia getting the drop on her if that were the case. Instead, she waited but leaned forward to gain easier access to the .380 she possessed.

Felicia turned, pulled off into the open field, and killed the engine of the vehicle. She turned her attention toward Monica again. "Well?" she stated.

"Well what?" Monica retorted.

Felicia shook her head and let out a light chuckle. "Are you going to get out or what, bitch?"

Monica couldn't tell whether Felicia was serious or joking. Her demeanor was hard to read. "Are you?" Monica asked matter-of-factly.

The two of them were now engrossed in an eye lock. Felicia's eyes lowered. She shook her head for a second time. "Fine." Felicia grabbed hold of the car handle, opened the driver's door, and climbed out.

Monica studied her with a watchful eye. She still contemplated drawing her gun.

Felicia spun around, surprising Monica. "Are you gonna get out or are you staying here?"

There was a brief pause before Monica spoke. "Of course I'm going to get out." Monica tried to hide her nervousness through laughter.

"Well, let's go then!" Felicia slammed the driver's door shut.

Monica let out a deep sigh and exited the vehicle. She watched as Felicia snatched off the wig she was wearing and tossed it in the car along with the clothes she wore. Monica followed suit.

"Go get in the car," Felicia instructed Monica.

By now, Monica had retrieved her .380 and moved it to the front of her waist. She nodded at Felicia and made her way over to the luxury car. She was relieved to see that it was empty. The sudden explosion behind her caused Monica to jump as she opened the unlocked passenger door. She hopped in the Benz and watched Felicia scurry over to the car as the car they had just exited went up in a blaze.

Moments later, Felicia was doing a hundred miles per hour in the direction from which they had just come.

Felicia was the first to break the silence now that they were miles away from the site. "Are you okay?" she asked.

"Yeah, I'm fine. Are you?" Monica returned.

"As good as can be," Felicia lied.

If she only knew, thought Felicia as she pushed her Benz CLS 350. Her mind shifted to the disturbing message she'd received earlier. She couldn't help but replay it in her head. The words, *"Trust no one,"* had Felicia all the way on point.

Chapter 5

Thomas McCarthy removed his suit jacket and necktie as he paced the ICU hallway of the Sunrise Hospital & Medical Center. It had been almost three hours since they had arrived and neither the doctors nor nurses had given him any kind of information. They weren't even allowed in the special emergency room. He and his wife were forced to watch as the medical staff members spilled in and out of their daughter's room.

Linda McCarthy was a very emotionally strong woman but seeing her child in the condition she was in was enough to break any mother down. Maternally, she felt helpless. She sat in the empty row of chairs with tearful eyes while watching her husband pace back and forth, making her even more nervous. The only other time she had seen him so worried was the day she had actually given birth to Charlie. He must've eventually realized it, because after catching sight of her emotional state, he calmed down and sat next to his wife. Agent McCarthy interlaced his right hand's fingers with hers, and kissed her knuckles. They both just sat there without saying a word, wondering the same thing: was their child even still alive?

After what seemed like an eternity, finally the doctor exited the glassless double doors and walked straight in front of Tom and Linda. They both stood immediately as if the judge had just entered the courtroom. Dr. Chi removed his blue latex gloves and tucked them into the

outer pockets of his white surgical smock. He pulled off
the matching hat and then unwrapped the surgical mask
from his face, revealing an untrustworthy smile.

"Hi. I'm Dr. Chi." The Japanese man introduced himself in perfectly good English. "I'm sorry it took so long.
Honestly, it required every available resource we had
to revive her, and then stabilize her. She's doing a little
better now."

His words were music to the McCarthys' ears. They
listened attentively.

"Her heart rate is very low, but at least it's steady for
the moment. Her pulse is faint and she's being helped to
breathe by a machine. She's being placed on a respirator
as we speak, but she is alive. However, we will need to
have her under observation for the next forty-eight hours
due to the severity and nature of her illness."

Tom appreciated Dr. Chi's straightforwardness. Linda
buried her face in her husband's chest as he struggled to
hold his composure himself. He knew he had to remain
strong for his wife as well as for his little girl.

"Is she conscious?" he asked with a knot in his throat.

"I'm afraid not. She probably won't be for quite some
time." Dr. Chi figured that this was the best time to fill
them in on the rest of the horrific news. "Her condition
is very rare; in fact, less than 2.6 percent of people in the
world have ever experienced this."

"In America, this year?" Tom asked.

"In the recorded history of the world," the doctor
corrected.

Tom and Linda's eyes widened at the same time.

"What? How did this happen?" Tom asked, cringing as
he awaited the answer.

"We are running some more tests now to see. I assure
you, you have the best doctors available to you now. And
they will do everything within their power to see to it that

your daughter gets the best medical attention possible. A lot of tests have been run during the past two hours. Mr. McCarthy, I do have to be honest with you about one thing. At the very least, your daughter will need a bone marrow transplant by someone with a very rare blood type that is not encountered by traditional blood drives. And this entire procedure is very costly. So costly that she needs nothing but the best experts from around the world at her side. We will keep her here and do what we can, for as long as we can. But we're limited. For the time being, she is about to be transported to a special ward where you'll be able to see her very shortly, but not for long. You have to be very strong for your daughter, and for yourselves. All you can really do now is pray," the doctor concluded.

Both Tom and Linda McCarthy looked at each other. They knew the doctor's last statement was nothing but the truth. Linda McCarthy extended her hand. Tom McCarthy took hold of his wife's hand and pulled her into his embrace.

Chapter 6

Bubbles drove the burgundy Porsche Cayenne with Sparkle riding shotgun, ready for whatever, while Glitter sat in the back checking her weapon. Two Ducatis with armed Double Gs drove in back of them, keeping their distance, but staying close enough to protect them in case of an ambush of any sort. It was close to 4:00 a.m. Their destination: one of the warehouses they used for meeting places and drop-offs. Tonight, they were to meet up with the Spalding brothers.

"There they go right there," Sparkle pointed out after noticing a navy blue van parked on the side of the abandoned warehouse.

Bubbles put on her hazard lights, signaling for the two Ducatis that trailed them to speed up ahead and circle the area. The Cayenne slowed down until the Ducatis returned, facing their direction head-on, flashing their high beams as they passed and did a U-turn.

Bubbles noticed only four out of the five Spalding brothers were standing in the back when they arrived. Each of them was chain-smoking a different brand of cigarettes. They looked tremendously nervous as the Cayenne pulled up with the bikers. Bubbles hopped out of the driver's side followed by Glitter and Sparkle.

"Where's Mike?" Bubbles asked with authority.

Both Glitter and Sparkle stood on opposite sides of Bubbles with their weapons drawn and cocked. They had heard about the infamous Spalding brothers.

They had reputations for being the most ruthless and grimiest dudes in all Las Vegas, so they weren't taking any chances.

"Well, hello to you too, big and sexy," Randy Spalding replied.

Bubbles rolled her eyes. "Where's your brother?" she repeated.

"Not here." He snorted. "He's still shook up pretty badly, you know. After all, she was one of y'all. He didn't want to take any chances," Randy Spalding replied while stepping on his lit cigarette as he blew a long stream of smoke from his lungs.

Bubbles peered over at the other three brothers, who all had guns tucked in their waistbands. "The agreement was that you all be here," she reminded them.

Frazier, Jesse, and Mark emerged from the shadows of the building with six full duffel bags that landed at the feet of Bubbles, Glitter, and Sparkle. The total was $462,000.

"Look, sweetheart, it's all there. We held up our end of the deal. Just remember, the way a hit usually works is the actual assassins are the ones who get the bags of money. We're not used to all this blackmailing shit," Randy Spalding spat.

The deal he had made with the Double Gs had left him uneasy. They were done robbing banks and killing people, at least until their trial was over, but he knew his and his brothers' options were limited. It was either agree to their terms or go to war with the entire Double Gs organization and risk the footage the Double Gs possessed being leaked of them kidnapping and torturing a powerful figure, and of their brother Mike being sodomized by one of the Double Gs. That was the real reason he had told his brother sit this one out. He knew how much of a hothead he was and he didn't want to jeopardize everything in case Mike flew off the handle halfcocked when they got in front of some of the women responsible for their predicament. The only thing in their favor was that Diamond Morgan, the best criminal attorney in the area, agreed to represent them on their pending case.

"Just make sure y'all hold up y'all end of the bargain and we win our trial," Jesse roared.

"Yeah," Mark instigated. "And give the lovely Ms. Morgan a kiss for me."

His Irish accent really annoyed Glitter. If looks could kill, there'd only be three Spalding brothers present instead of four.

Mark Spalding caught Glitter's grilling stare. "You like what you see, thick mama?" he joked.

"Not at all. I don't like the look of shit," Glitter spat.

"What the fuck did you just say to me?" Mark Spalding reached down to his waistband.

"I wish you would, you fuckin' leprechaun!" Sparkle boomed, coming to her sister's defense.

The sound of her AK-47 assault rifle being cocked stopped Mark Spalding in his tracks. His hand never made it to the butt of his weapon. By now Glitter had both her Glocks drawn and cocked. The two youngest Spalding brothers froze in time. They knew they were not quick enough on the draw to pull out without getting cut down by the assault rifle and Glocks the twins waved around. Even if they could have, they knew they were no match for the cavalry that had appeared out of nowhere. The Ducatis pulled up back to back, brandishing huge-caliber weapons.

"Whoa now!" Randy Spalding bellowed. "Everybody just take it easy." He smiled, revealing a mouthful of stained teeth that suffered from too many cigarettes and coffee.

The entire time, Bubbles never flinched. She calmly spoke, "It's okay, girls." Bubbles held up her right hand. All the Double Gs immediately stood down but remained on high alert.

"Fellas, relax," Randy Spalding told his brothers. "Everything's fine."

"No, everything is not fine," Bubbles corrected him. "As you should know, we don't take too kindly to anybody disrespecting us." She directed her attention to Mark Spalding. "But a simple apology will make this all go away and everybody can go on their merry way."

Mark Spalding frowned. "Apology?"

Before he could say something that would make the situation go from zero to a hundred, Randy Spalding interjected. "Apologize to the lady," he instructed his brother.

"Jesus H. Christ, Randy!" Mark Spalding contested.

"Do it, goddammit."

Mark Spalding clenched his teeth. He was growing tired of the Double Gs. In his mind, he was all too ready for war, but he knew he'd be fighting a losing battle. He prayed for the day when things would be different and the tables were turned. For now, he knew he had to submit. "My deepest apologies," he chimed right before he stormed over to the van.

Glitter didn't even acknowledge the gesture but she respected the fact that Bubbles defended her honor. It was situations such as this one that made Glitter proud to be a part of such an organization.

"You fellas enjoy the rest of your day," Bubbles concluded.

Two of the bikers scurried over to their side and retrieved the duffle bags. They loaded the Cayenne with the bags of money then hopped back on their bikes.

Bubbles, Glitter, and Sparkle all backpedaled to the Porsche truck. Within minutes, the SUV and bikes had vanished into thin air. The four brothers watched as their taillights disappeared into the distance.

"Them fucking fat whores gonna get what they deserve!" Mark Spalding barked. They were all joined in a huddle, each lighting another cigarette.

"What were you trying to do here, get us all freaking killed?" Frazier Spalding questioned.

"Fuck them!" Mark Spalding said. "The first chance I get I'm going to rip one of those dyke bitches' hearts out and feed it to the dogs!" he stated.

"You and me both, brother," Randy Spalding agreed while Frazier and Jesse Spalding gave agreeing nods. "But first we have to get our situation taken care of. I hope this plan of Mike's really works," Randy added.

"Yeah. If it doesn't, consider us fucked, literally," Mark seriously joked. Needless to say, none of the others laughed.

Chapter 7

Saturday night had come around again. The usual partygoers who got dressed to impress and shined their rides headed downtown to the usual spots they knew would be jumping. Many of them were highly disappointed as they pulled up between the two most popular clubs in the city of Las Vegas. Although Club Treasures was very much still alive, Club Panties was closed down, boarded up, and sealed off with tape. So the energy that used to be balanced was extremely lopsided.

Only one side of the wide street was pumping. The long lines of hundreds of beautiful women across the street were absent. The motorcycle stunt shows were nonexistent. The Escalades' presidential grand entrance never happened. The battle of the sexes never took place. For most of both clubs' regular attendants, the real action had always been outside. Bright lights used to be everywhere. Only the elite used to have a place to park their $100,000 machines. But tonight, anyone could pull up and park anywhere they wanted. Maseratis were next to Toyotas and scooters were next to Harleys. It just wasn't right.

Initially, Club Treasures' owner, Sammy, was happy that he would finally own all of the business in the area. When he was first approached with the proposition, his first thought was that he wouldn't live long enough to enjoy the outcome if he agreed. But once he made it past a full seven days with no backlash, he was convinced he was in the clear as being a snitch and he killed three birds with one stone: one, his competition; two, the eighty grand gambling debt he had with Prime; three, the early termination of his probation.

The feds held up their end of the deal, keeping his name secure, Sammy believed. It was his secret tip, given to him by Prime, that tipped them off that drugs were being sold and prostitution was being offered inside of Club Panties. He had photos to support his claim, compliments of Prime. Sammy didn't know what Prime had against the Double Gs and he really didn't care, but he quickly learned a valuable lesson about doing any more business with him. Sammy believed that with Club Panties out of the way, all of the action would come to his side of the street; but yesterday and that evening were proving that his theory couldn't be further from the truth.

No matter how much the DJ tried to liven up the spot, or how much they promoted on Las Vegas Boulevard, people still only came in and left after a few drinks. Club Treasures quickly became just a local bar. Even the third-level VIP lounge was empty. The strippers were still fully clothed, sitting in the dressing room, filing their nails and doing their hair, still waiting for big names and entourages to be announced. It just wasn't happening.

Sammy sat back in his office chair rubbing his pudgy belly while shaking his head deep in thought. He had lost a lot of money in a week's time. He had gone from making over a hundred grand a night, four nights out of the week, to barely making $50,000 an entire week. And it was all his fault. After he let Prime sucker him into doing his dirty work, he and his crew hadn't stepped foot back up in his establishment. He may have not been the sharpest knife in the bunch, but he wasn't the dullest one, either, Sammy concluded. It didn't take for him to be a rocket scientist to realize that with an overhead and spending habit like the one, he had he needed to think of something quick, real quick.

Chapter 8

The all-black, tinted Chrysler 300C was rarely driven, and when it was it usually meant trouble for somebody. But tonight, he was just driving it as a means of keeping a low profile. It meant his plan was either taking off in the right direction, or falling apart. And he needed to know which one.

He drove straight up Flamingo Road until he was about to approach the highway ramp. He turned into the gas station truck stop rest area and circled the lot until he saw what he was looking for. Just as he had hoped, it was parked at the end closest to the airport. He cut his headlights off and parked right behind the silver SL550. He flashed his high beams into the back windshield twice.

The SL driver's side door opened slowly. He watched as a single stiletto stuck out and planted itself onto the ground. Shortly after, the rest of her body followed. She shut the door and activated the alarm. He smiled and chuckled as he watched her nervously scan the lot while shifting the strands of the fake blond wig she wore. She pulled her black trench coat tightly across her chest as she rushed to the passenger side of the Chrysler. She removed her dark Chanel shades after getting in, hoping she wasn't followed.

No words were spoken for the first few seconds. Prime just sat staring Monica in her eyes. Based on her eyes, he assumed she was scared. *She has to be,* he reasoned to himself. *Why else would she have agreed to come?* he concluded. They had spoken numerous times over the phone, and had even been communicating through texts, which they both deleted afterward. But this was their first time physically meeting since their first and last encounter.

Before they went any further, Prime felt that there was something that he needed to know. "Did you do it?" he asked with a stern tone.

Monica quickly turned her head away and stared out of the window. "No," she whispered over her left shoulder, but then spun back around to face him.

"She did." Her voice heightened. "Felicia did it. I stood there and watched. I held that little girl. She dropped the doll after watching her mother getting shot in the head. I held her; and then, before I could blink, her body slipped from my grip. I didn't even notice Felicia turned the gun on her. That's how quick it all happened. I can't believe she did that." Her voice lowered. "We did that," she corrected herself. She leaned over and plunged her face into the right shoulder of Prime's black body.

He wrapped his arm around her and held her as she cried. "Relax. It's okay. It's done. It's over with." Prime used her vulnerability to his advantage. "But you're staying with me tonight. You can't let them see you like this. You see what they did to y'all homegirl Careese." He drove the nail in the coffin. "If they ever found out about us . . ."

His words resonated in Monica's mind. *How did I get here?* she asked herself. She knew she was in too deep without a life preserver. She had compromised her position long ago by sleeping with not one suspect but two under federal investigation. Her thoughts were disrupted by the sudden movement of Prime. He released her from his body.

"You a'ight?"

"Yes, I'm fine," she replied, clearing her throat.

"Oh, a'ight. You had zoned out for a minute."

Monica flashed a fake smile. "Just go please."

Prime stared at her for a moment. He snickered and threw his car in drive. She reclined her seat as the car slowly pulled off.

"If Only for One Night" by Luther Vandross began to play. To Monica, Prime was so mysteriously intriguing. *But he's a criminal,* she reminded herself. Still, she was drawn to his fearlessness. She would never forget the way he stepped in between Esco's and Clips's guns back in Club Treasures. The way he had defused the heated potential altercation spoke volumes about his confidence and status in the streets as a boss. She was attracted to men like Prime, minus the street life. She believed he was an alpha by the way he had handled the situation and her. *If only things were different, he were different.* But for tonight, she needed to face a different truth. Too much was at stake for her to slip up. She was closer than she ever was. Mistakes from here on out would only be detrimental. Careese Pearson was certainly evidence of that.

As Prime drove, he thought about how well the situation was unfolding. It was happening. He was on the inside, at next to no cost. It was a dream come true. He thought he was finally ahead of the game again. To him, the total outcome all depended on how he played out the night. He felt that he had to make Monica feel comfortable and strong again. Strong enough to head right back into the lion's den, smelling like fresh vegetables instead of raw steak.

The Chrysler rode the shoulder lane until it turned onto the highway off the exit ramp. Monica had no idea of where she was, or how far they had come. She didn't care. She just wanted to get away from it all. Even if it was only for one night.

The deep suburban residential streets were long and wide. The traffic lights were spread far apart. Not many vehicles were on the road at such a late hour. Monica stayed just as alert as Prime. They both kept their eyes rotating between the rearview and side-view mirrors for the entire ride, especially as it started to come to an end.

Prime turned off of the main strip and navigated his way through the smoothly paved back roads. Every piece of property he passed seemed to outdo the one prior. The scenery was peaceful. The car finally eased up off the gas and rode the brake before slowly turning into a four-car garage driveway, and parking into the third slot. The exterior of the mini-mansion was overly impressive. The lawn was fresh green as if it had all just grown in this morning. It was outlined with exotic flower gardens and miniature statue fountains. The outside of the house had long, wide glass windows that sat in the middle of the stone walls. A single brass-railed balcony wrapped around all four sides of the upper level.

Inside the garage, Monica got out next to the chrome Hummer on her right. Prime escaped from between the Chrysler and the snow white Porsche Panorama. He reached for Monica's hand and led her past the candy apple red Ferrari F50. They exited the garage through a regular door, and strolled up the multicolored stone steps. Prime punched in a code to unlock the black steel gate that protected the front door. He stuck his keys into the lock and pushed it wide open, pausing before he entered, as if he was listening for anything unusual. He reached back for Monica's hand and led her through the darkness. The lights automatically came on due to the motion sensors detecting his presence. The entire house was wired that way. He led her across the Persian carpet, to the long, circular black suede sofa. She set her purse on the octagon-shaped glass coffee table in the center, where many subscription sports magazines were neatly aligned in chronological order.

"I'll be right back. Make yourself comfortable," Prime whispered. He disappeared into one of the three hallways that were next to the spiral staircase that led up to the open upper level. She counted out the six rooms that she could see. The lights suddenly went back out as music began to play. It all startled Monica. There weren't any signs of speakers anywhere in sight, but she was surrounded by Alicia Keys's "Un-Thinkable (I'm Ready)" playing as the plasma flat screen on the wall across from her turned on, showing a virtual fireplace. Seconds later, Prime returned with two glasses and a bottle of red wine. He set them on the coffee table and stood up tall to help Monica remove her coat, wig, and shades.

"Relax," he ordered in a seductive voice. "You act like you've never been here before. You're safe here. I can promise you that." Prime flashed her a grin.

If he only knew. I don't remember a damn thing, Monica thought.

Prime leaned in and kissed her lips. She tensed up but Prime's tongue parted her mouth and probed its insides. Monica embraced the kiss. Prime slid his hand up Monica's blouse and bra with one hand and slithered his other one up her skirt. Monica could feel his hardness pressed up against her outer thigh. She reached down for it and began to massage him. Prime toyed with her nipple while he parted and probed Monica's thick inner thighs. The fact that she wore no panties gave him easy access to her moist tunnel.

Up until the night they had officially met, Monica had only had three sexual encounters in her life. First in college, second was Prime, and Starr was her last. All three experiences were drastically different. Although she couldn't remember much from the first night with Prime, her body recalled the passionate aggression of being tossed around and manhandled in the most captivating way. The yearning for more stuck with her for days after.

She rotated her hips and embraced Prime's fingers. She tossed her head back and closed her eyes as he trailed down to her neck. While he sucked on her neck and fondled her seductively, out of nowhere an image of Starr appeared in Monica's head. Her eyes shot open. Prime sensed the sudden change and paused.

"I can't," Monica announced. Although it was all just an act, she was about to violate the Double Gs' code for a second time: no penetration. For some odd reason, she felt some sense of loyalty and love for the Double Gs, or was it for Starr? She questioned herself. Monica made an attempt to rise up but Prime grabbed hold of her legs.

"Just chill," he offered. "I got you." Prime wrapped his right hand around Monica's back and pulled her in closer to him as they locked lips again.

She made a failed attempt to resist and became engulfed in the kiss. Monica was all in. She reached for the bottom of his Polo shirt along with his wife beater, all in one motion pulling them over his head. Her eyes traced the outline of his bare chest, his six pack, and the elastic band of his silk boxers. She reached in to unbuckle his pants as he stood up in front of her, letting it all drop down to his ankles. She opened her eyes wider as she watched his penis grow until it pointed inches away from her face. She gripped it with both hands, and held it, feeling the warmth penetrate her palms as the blood in the thick veins flowed to his shaft. She pointed it upward and scanned his sack. She couldn't help but lean forward and kiss around it. She let the point of her tongue point out to taste it. She took the time to figure it out. She decided to just hold it steady with her left hand, and let her imagination fill in the blanks as she reached under her skirt and fingered herself with her right hand. She slipped the tip of his dick in her mouth and sucked it to make it moist. Sucking turned into licking and licking turned into deep-throating. She freed her pussy-soaked fingers and spread her own lubrication all over his inches until it smelled of her feminine scent. She opened her mouth wide and stuck her tongue out until the pulsating heat of his manhood squeezed between her tonsils and defeated her gag reflex. She rested her stretched tongue against his scrotum and firmly clamped her jaws down.

Prime stood there staring down at the top of her head. He clenched his teeth as he watched her work him like he had never been worked before. He was almost unable to stand. He placed both of his hands on the back of her head, trying to maintain his balance.

Feeling him do so made Monica take charge even more. She sucked with intense passion. Prime was struggling not to release so soon but Monica was making it hard for him. She kept sucking until he couldn't take it any longer.

The explosion nearly caused his legs to buckle. His thick, hot juice burst in Monica's mouth and slammed in the back of her throat. Still, Monica wouldn't let up. She felt his rock hardness softening. She attacked his shaft vigorously. Seconds later it became hard as steel again.

Prime palmed her forehead and forcefully shoved it away from his abdominal section as he pulled away. Monica fell backward toward the couch with a lustful smile glued to her face.

She knew she had done her job, but knew it was far from over. She cocked her legs wide open and bent her knees in the air away from each other. Her dripping sex invited Prime in.

Prime towered over Monica, looking down at her. He wrapped both of his long arms and huge hands around her neck and lowered his head between her legs. He dropped to his knees and applied slight pressure to her neck.

She raised her hips up to meet his face as he tightened his grip. Monica had never felt such an adrenaline rush. She could barely even breathe. She gripped both of his wrists with the soft palms of her own hands as he squeezed her neck even harder. She rode his face, grinding her erect clitoris against his teasing tongue. She planted the heel of the stiletto deep into his back muscles, just to be able to raise her waist up higher as he sucked up her juices like water from the last cactus in the center of the Sahara Desert.

Her face began to turn red. Black spots appeared before her eyes, blurring her vision. She began to wrestle herself away from him, acting as if she was trying to escape his grasp, but she really wasn't. It was actually turning her on. She wanted more. Much more. She felt an orgasm arising and gyrated her hips in a circular motion to enhance the pleasure. Finally, Monica sprayed her fire and desire all over Prime's tongue, coating his full lips with the evidence of her sinful pleasure.

Prime tried to slurp up every drop. He released his hands from her neck and gripped a tight hold of her thin waist. Without warning, he plunged his dick inside of her.

Monica screamed from the intoxicating pain that was intensely invited. She rocked her hips back and forth as he sank himself deeper into her. Prime thrust and long dicked her, in attempts to loosen up Monica's inner walls that welcomed every inch of him. It was Prime now; he could feel the sensation forming within his body. His down stroke increased as he prepared himself for a second orgasm. Monica was caught up in the matrix. Intimacy had never felt so good to her. She felt Prime plunging deeper inside her cave.

"Oh, yes. Right there," she cried as she dug her nails into Prime's sides. Her words shot straight to Prime's dick. Within seconds, the both of them reached the point of no return simultaneously. Prime let out a loud grunt. Monica's cries were of pure ecstasy. Prime released himself inside of Monica and she did nothing to stop him. They were both savoring the moment.

Prime rolled off of Monica and lay on his back. Monica slid over and curled up underneath Prime. She rested her head on his bare chest. He placed his hand on top of her head and began to stroke her hair. Monica closed her eyes. Her life and everything that led up to that moment flashed before her very eyes. She had slipped into deep thought.

For the life of her, she couldn't understand or believe how messy she had gotten with the case, her career, the Double Gs, and now Prime. Slowly but surely, she felt herself losing control and focus of the main objective: to make Starrshma Fields and the Double Gs pay for all of the mayhem they were responsible for in the Las Vegas area. She had been living a lifestyle that she was unfamiliar with for so long that it was starting to take its toll on her. She could feel herself slipping. She questioned whether she was in too deep. So many thoughts invaded her mind. *How the hell am I going to get myself up out of all of this?* was her last thought before she drifted off to sleep.

Chapter 9

During the past few years, Freeze was considered to be one of the most feared gangsters in the city. He usually took the number one spot of everyone's list because he constantly made extreme examples. And even though today was a beautiful day, it would be no different. Being that they had most of the city sewn up, regular cops didn't come to his territory under any circumstances. Especially when he was physically out. His soldiers had been trained to fire on any police car, on sight. The police quickly got the message. An underpaid eight-hour shift wasn't worth dying for.

Usually, the average person who chose the street life had to choose whether he wanted to be an ultimate hustler or a notorious gangster. He mastered the act of being both. There were only two obstacles in his way of being virtually indestructible: the Double Gs and Prime. There definitely wasn't enough room for all three of them to exist in the same city, thought Freeze. Not even the same state. It was time for the process of elimination to begin, was Freeze's frame of mind as of late. With all that was going on in the city, he knew it was the perfect time. At any moment he was expecting his most trusted comrade.

Esco had been loyal to Freeze since they were in the juvenile detention center. He was the type who went all out when it was time to prove himself. He stood up for everybody who was with him and he would jump on the front line to go against the opposition. He admired and respected Esco's character. He taught Esco most of what he knew in the game and told him mostly everything he needed to know to become his successor one day. There were just a few parts of his life that he couldn't let Esco in on yet, if ever.

The money green CLS 600 pulled up and parked in front of the corner store on their main drug strip. It was a narrow one-way street, the slums. The houses were run-down, and most of them were abandoned, excluding the dopefiends and homeless people living in them. The sidewalks were badly chipped and unlevel. In some spots, entire slabs of cement were missing. The streets them-selves were the worst. Cars had to drive extremely slowly to prevent the rims on their rides from being cracked.

Freeze sat in the passenger seat and reclined as far as he could lean back. His black and silver L.A. Raiders fitted cap was pulled low over his eyes. After Freeze broke down the plan to him, Esco put his car in reverse and headed to their intended destination.

Chapter 10

Linda and Tom McCarthy were escorted to a higher private floor of the medical center. They were both taking the news extremely hard. They wondered how such a tragedy could be happening to them. Charlie was so innocent. She had been nothing less than a sweetheart since she was a baby, thought Linda and Tom. They began to blame it on the karma of their professions. Tom more so.

Tom had his phone shut off the entire time since he had left his colleague's funeral, so he was sealed off from what had been happening in the outside world. But as he and Linda were escorted to a more private and comfortable waiting room, he couldn't escape it.

In the far corner, the television showed rerun clips of the funeral. Tom and Linda McCarthy watched their daughter fall from her chair, in shock. The next newsflash shocked Tom McCarthy even more.

"What the hell!" he chimed.

The words BANK ROBBERY below the photo of the woman that appeared on the screen caused McCarthy's eyes to widen. He instantly recognized the woman as Careese Pearson, former member of the Double Gs gang.

Agent McCarthy filled with anger as his law enforcement instincts kicked back in. He knew it was an executed hit the second he tuned in. Linda's distraught attention was also directed to the television's wide screen as she watched the video surveillance footage being replayed.

They both drew closer to the television and took a seat.
Tom and Linda McCarthy clung to the reporter's words
of the next segment. Tears filled Linda McCarthy's eyes
as she listened.

Officer Douglass's family picture was shown while the
newscaster recapped the chilling events that had taken
place. She buried her face in Tom's chest as the picture
of Cameron Douglass, who seemed to be nearly the same
age as their beloved angel, Charlie, flashed on the screen.
The scene was a reminder of the possibility of having to
bury her own daughter.

McCarthy listened attentively to the witnesses who
were interviewed. It was the Douglass family's elderly
next-door neighbor who could only recall two female
agents pulling up, parking in their shared driveway,
entering the house, and then leaving. Tom smelled a
setup and it had the name Double Gs all over it. To the
world, it looked like the FBI took revenge for what had
happened to Agents Craven and Mullin. It was a complete mockery of law enforcement, thought McCarthy.

He was so engrossed in his own thoughts that he had
completely forgotten where he was, and why he was there.
He released his wife's warm hand and jumped up. There
was no doubt in her mind what was running through her
husband's head.

"Just go. I'll call you if anything changes," she encouraged her husband.

Tom McCarthy ran his palm alongside his wife's face
then cupped her chin. "I love you," he said, right before
he leaned in and kissed her on the lips.

Tom McCarthy then made his way to the hallway
door. He was stopped in his tracks by Dr. Chi's presence.
The way he entered the room mixed with his facial
expression caused Agent McCarthy's heart to drop into
the pit of his stomach.

Chapter 11

Felicia's R1 pulled up to the front of Diamond's high-rise loft and parked around the back. She understood the professional image that Diamond always upheld, so she left the helmet and motorcycle jacket on the back seat, fixed her hair and clothes, and strutted through the front door like the lady she was. She greeted the doorman as she passed him. She approached the front desk and signed in the logbook as the desk attendant phoned upstairs to confirm her arrival. The doorman then escorted her to the elevator.

The elevator doors reopened directly into Diamond's huge, luxurious duplex apartment. It was early in the morning. The sun was just beginning to spill in the through the single wall-length window that provided a picture-perfect view of the city.

"Good morning," Diamond greeted her as she slowly footed her way downstairs wearing nothing but her robe and slippers. "Have a seat. I'll be right with you," she welcomed Felicia.

Felicia came in and flopped down onto the bright red oval-shaped sofa. She looked up at all of the expensive art paintings that covered the walls. Every one of them was either misunderstood by her or old-fashioned ugly.

"So, how did it go?" Diamond asked as she sat down on the edge of the royal blue armless love seat directly across from Felicia. Her words came out somewhat dry. "Aside from the seven o'clock news version, of course, "she added with a little sarcasm in her tone.

Felicia hesitated. "She did well."

"So, she was the one who actually killed them?" Diamond wanted to know.

"Absolutely," Felicia lied. It was actually she who had put the gun right to the mother's head and then dragged both of the bodies back into the living room. She had even sat them on the couch and positioned them to make it look like they were watching television.

"So where's she at now?" Diamond inquired.

Felicia shrugged her shoulders. "At first she was cool after we left. I guess it hadn't settled in yet. But then I think it started to hit her pretty hard. My guess is she's cool. She just had to shake it off."

"And what about you?" Diamond asked as she crossed her massive legs.

"I'm good. I'm pretty sure by now I've seen it all, at least twice. Some things I've gotten used to. Some I never will."

"And where does today fit in?" Diamond was so used to probing the minds of others without them even noticing.

Felicia answered, "I might not have agreed with the method but I believe in the cause. The message. It had to be done."

"Exactly. Now let's make sure our girl understands that."

"I'm sure she does," Felicia replied.

Diamond released a half smile. "So anyway, I went by the club. It's a mess."

"I'm sure it is."

"Yeah, I couldn't stand to look at it."

"Did Starr see it yet? And, where is she?" Felicia asked.

"No, she didn't want to. I dropped her off at one of the houses. She said she wanted to collect her thoughts alone before we made any other moves. I have the Spalding brothers' case coming up next week so I'll be going over paperwork for the rest of the week anyway, so I let her be," Diamond replied.

"Makes sense," Felicia offered.

Diamond let out a light chuckle. "Yeah, but what doesn't make sense to me is the fact that I've had to hear about a freak session at the club during the raid."

Felicia was unfazed by her statement. "It wasn't what you think, though." Felicia spoke in a solemn manner. "Starr wanted to test Monica."

Diamond knew she had displayed more emotions than she intended. Initially, she had no intent of bringing it up, but it had been eating at her ever since she had watched the footage. The last thing she wanted to do was alarm Felicia and have her running back to Starr, or alarm her about anything for that matter.

"I get it," she retorted.

"Is everything okay?" Felicia asked. She felt Diamond was acting kind of strange. She wasn't sure how much she had heard or what all she knew, but whatever it was had her acting different.

Diamond sensed that Felicia was reading her. "Don't think I'm hatin' on ol' girl or anything. It ain't like Starr and I are exclusive. You know, we just have a li'l fun," Diamond downplayed her relationship with Starr. The fact of the matter was that she was deeply in love with Starr. No one really knew how strongly she felt for Starrshma Fields, not even Starr herself.

She noticed Felicia staring at her oddly. She knew she was assessing her to see where her head was at. It took all of her power to keep her composure. She was tempted to mention what all she had seen on the video footage to see how Felicia would react to her discovery, but she sided against it. The timing wasn't right. She was waiting on her inside source to return to her with vital details. Until then, she would just watch and see how things played out.

She instantly switched subjects. "Starr said she would be calling a meeting as soon as she decided on a meeting place."

"Cool. I'll just wait to hear from either one of you." Felicia stood up.

Diamond looked up at her from where she sat. Her mind drifted off elsewhere. So much was on her mind. So many secrets. So many lies. So many responsibilities. Diamond's trance was broken by the sound of Felicia's booming voice.

"Huh?" She stared at Felicia.

"I said, are you sure you're okay?" Felicia asked a second time.

"Yeah. I'm straight. Just tired, that's all." It was true. She was tired, but not in the sense of not being rested enough. Diamond was more tired of all of the bullshit that surrounded her and the organization she loved. "Tomorrow, I'll be as good as new." She smiled.

"I hope so. I'm not used to seeing you like this," Felicia stated. "Hopefully tomorrow will be a better day for all of us," Felicia added.

That was wishful thinking because tomorrow was not promised to either one of them.

Chapter 12

Starr veered off Highway 159 onto Charleston Boulevard. She hadn't realized she had product with nothing to roll it in at her place until after Diamond had dropped her off and was long gone. She dreaded having to drive herself to the store nearest to her ranch home in Calico Basin, but since her release from federal custody she was in dire need of a blunt, so she took the drive. Very seldom did she smoke, but the dozen times she had in her lifetime were all for good reason, she concluded.

Starr traveled back in time to her first two encounters with the drug. The first time was after she had witnessed a man rape and kill a woman, when she was sixteen, over ten dollars he claimed she had stolen from him. The second was when she had just passed her initiation to become a Double G. Starr knew the exotic weed she intended to roll would help ease her mind so she could strategize her next moves.

There was no doubt in her mind that there was more heat right around the corner; and time was of the essence. Ever since the crooked cop Officer Douglass had snitched on his partner, Blake, and the federal agents had been slain, all eyes had been on her. They had come for her and they had come hard. As she thought of how they had destroyed the Double Gs club, Starr grimaced as she rode home from the store, past the Red Rock Canyon national state park, and turned onto her multimillion dollar property. She loved Club Panties and felt a sense of loss. She knew they really didn't have anything on her to warrant tearing it up. She believed they were mad behind the federal agents' deaths and wanted to send her a message loud and clear.

Her attention was drawn to the ringing of her phone. She frowned when she looked down and saw who the caller was. There was only one person who had been calling her from this type of number. "Yeah," Starr answered dryly.

The anonymous caller let out a light chuckle.

"Look, I don't—"

"No, you look!" The anonymous caller cut Starr short. "I'm calling to do yo' ass a favor, on the hip, again." The anonymous caller put emphasis on his last word in an annoyed tone.

Starr was unfazed by both the caller's words and tone."Don't do me no fuckin' favors, muthafucka!" She spat venom.

The anonymous caller chuckled for a second time. Only, this time, his laughter grew louder with each chuckle. "Suit yourself." His tone was nonchalant. "Your freedom."

Starr had just pulled up to her ranch home and put her A5 in park in frustration. She was just about fed up with the games, but something about the way the anonymous caller made his last statement stood out to her.

She could tell the caller hadn't hung up. "What about my freedom?" she was curious to know. She had already determined that the anonymous caller only called her when he had information.

"They're waiting for you. I told you, you have an informant in your crew. They have something else on you. It may be too late," the anonymous caller ended abruptly.

The next thing Starr heard was a dial tone. She couldn't believe her ears. She quickly tried to process her thoughts.

Something else on me? Starr played the words back in her head as she turned the key to the Audi sports car and put her hand on the gear shift. *What the fuck could they have on me?* she asked herself as she put her whip in reverse. Before Starr could back up, out of nowhere, her car was swarmed by a barrage of federal agents waving guns in her direction.

"Fuck!" Starr cursed. She threw the Audi back in park and complied with the orders for her to place her hands on the steering wheel. She couldn't help but smile at the anonymous caller's words. *"It may be too late."* The words danced in her mind. The caller was right, she concluded. The warning was too late. When her car door opened, her eyes grew cold at her first sight.

"Told ya I'd be seeing you soon," Agent Reddick announced sarcastically. The smug look on his face rubbed Starr in the worst way. The heat was hotter and closer than she had thought but, as Agent Reddick placed the handcuffs on her wrists, she was already thinking of ways to put out some, if not all, of the fires.

Chapter 13

The sound of the first muffled shot whistled through the air followed by the second. Both bodies dropped to the floor. The scene replayed in Monica's nightmare over and over until finally she willed herself to snap out of it. As she jumped out of her sleep, she realized the bed she was lying in wasn't her own.

The one night had turned into an entire weekend. It was early Monday morning. Monica sat up and looked around. Prime was nowhere to be found. She quickly reached down on the floor and retrieved her purse. She took out her personal cell phone and hopped up, running for the bathroom while dialing the number. She locked the door and sat on the toilet, listening to the ring pulse before he finally picked up, still half asleep.

"Hello," she said in the lowest voice she could. Before he could reply she began speaking in a hushed hurry. "Listen, I know you've been worried. I'm fine. I know you've seen some stuff on the news, but you have to believe—"

"I'm pulling you out," he calmly interrupted. "You're getting too deep."

"No," she forcefully interrupted. "I won't leave. I'm going to finish what I started. I'll check in with you later. Bye." She hung up. Just hearing his voice was reassuring enough. She wasn't alone in this. The two of them would singlehandedly dismantle the Double Gs together, as a team, seeking no credit for it. This was strictly personal.

And they were entirely too close to give up. They had spent too much time preparing for this to just let it all go to waste. She was the key and she wouldn't let him down. He had trained her too well.

The flip phone quickly slammed shut as she heard outside movement. Monica jumped up off of the toilet and flushed it, wondering what to do with the phone. All she had on was a pair of boy shorts. She put her right ear to the door and listened. The footsteps that were heard were moving farther away. It was her only chance. Monica ran the water briefly and then cut the lights out after tucking the phone into the back of her waistband. She cracked the door open and peeked through it. Prime was on the other side, standing in front of the TV, switching channels from *SportsCenter* to CNN.

Perfect, thought Monica. She swiftly made her way back into the bed and under the covers before he noticed. She eased the phone from behind her and dropped it down on the carpet next to her purse. Prime quickly turned to face her.

"Look who's up." He flashed a grin.

Monica matched his smile. *It's a shame I don't need him any longer,* she reasoned to herself. She was about to go in deeper than she had ever been and she didn't want to risk it all by communicating with him. She figured that by the time he realized that he was being spun, and left out of the loop, he'd be in jail or dead, the Double Gs would no longer exist, and Queen Fem would be destroyed. After all, Monica had her own personal plans and agenda for the "G" Files.

Chapter 14

Meanwhile, Across Town

Today was the big day. In less than a few hours, the courtroom would be packed with people for many different reasons. It was the beginning of one of the largest trials the city had seen in a full decade. For Diamond Morgan, she lived for such high-profile cases. Her name was already starting to be mentioned with the best of them: Cochran, Kardashian, Cutler, et cetera. She was feared. Fear was what made a great lawyer excellent, and an excellent lawyer fearless, and that summed up what Diamond Morgan was. That's what she had in her favor.

Her record reflected her hard-earned achievements. In her ten years of being a lawyer, she had won thirty-two trials, gotten twelve hung juries, and the one trial she did lose, she immediately got the conviction overturned and reversed on a direct appeal. They were acquitted on all charges and received a healthy settlement for wrongful imprisonment.

Although she had her game face on, she didn't feel like her "as cold as ice" self today. The last place she wanted to be was in a courtroom defending scum when they had the love of her life back in custody. It had been days and still she had been unable to have any contact or communication with Starr. When she had first received the anonymous call she thought it was a lie because none of her contacts or connects, from the attorney general's office down to mayor's office, seemed to know anything.

It wasn't until she drove out to Calico Basin that she realized there was some truth to the call.

As soon as the sun rose, Diamond had marched down to the federal building demanding to see her client, only to be spun by gibberish. The feds were using every trick in the book to delay the process of her seeing Starr. The only reason she was in court and not where they were holding Starr was because she knew Starr would have wanted her to stay the course and hold up their end of a deal the Double Gs had made. Diamond cleared her mind and tightened up her game face. *First thing first,* she told herself. *The Spalding brothers and Starr thereafter.*

Linda McCarthy had been up against Diamond a total of sixteen times. All sixteen times she had lost. She wanted this time to be different, and she believed it would be. But with Charlie's condition she hadn't had much time to prepare. She was distracted. Her head wasn't in it. She called up her best friend and colleague, Assistant U.S. Attorney Victoria Stockford. She was also a feared district attorney, much like Linda, only they defended the government's side, going up against criminals who thought they were above the laws, and broke them but claimed to be innocent.

After learning of Linda's personal family crisis, Victoria dropped everything to join her. She updated and briefed herself with every detail about the Spalding case over the entire weekend. She familiarized herself with every blatant piece of evidence that seemed to reinforce this seemingly open-and-shut case. She quickly became as ready as she would ever be. So ready that she had been the first person to show up to the courtroom. She had always heard about Diamond Morgan, especially from Linda, but she hadn't had the opportunity to match up against her. The time had finally come. "Chances make champions" was her frequently sung motto.

Linda made her way to the wood grain conference table that sat in the center of the room. She set her briefcase on it and opened it up next to the documents and files that were scattered all across it, appearing to be disorganized; but it was very much in order. Linda searched through a few of the files, and then walked off to the door that led to her actual private office. The room was much smaller and more comfortable. The drapes were closed, but the sun's rays outlined it, providing light. The floor was carpeted. A huge burgundy wood office desk sat in front of the window. A large leather chair sat behind it, facing the door. A two-seat leather sofa was placed on the opposite side. Two black metal file cabinets were on the right side of the door, and a burgundy wooden bookcase was on the left, taking up most of the wall with hundreds of law books. On her desk was a laptop, a conference phone, and framed photos of her family, mostly of Tom and Charlie. It was quiet. Peaceful. But it was still a battlefield where many wars had been lost, and even more were won.

Linda walked around to the back of the desk and picked up a close-up photo of Charlie, sporting the brightest smile missing her upper two front teeth. Linda kissed it as if it was actually Charlie. She took a few more seconds to meditate, and then exited the office.

Victoria was standing up, leaning over the table, packing the documents and files into both of their briefcases. She looked over at Linda and stood upright. "If you're not feeling up to this, I can—"

"No. I'm fine," Linda reassured her. "Once I get in the courtroom, trust me . . ."

"Medusa will appear," Victoria filled in, referring to Linda's nickname that most of the criminals gave her. It was a rumored myth that if you looked at D.A. McCarthy long enough you would turn to stone. That's how vicious

Linda was at what she did. Even in her defeat, she was the best. In just a few hours, she would display her best. With Victoria Stockford on her side, the odds of them being unbeatable were amplified.

Chapter 15

Somehow, Starr made it through the weekend. She was sure she was coming down with something. Her head throbbed, she felt somewhat lightheaded, and her mouth felt as if she was eating cotton, although she hadn't eaten a single thing that they tried to feed her since they had arrested her again. She wasn't sure whether they were trying to poison her, or at the very least did some pretty degrading things to the food, so she refused every meal, waiting to be set free, bailed out, or transferred to general population. She was surprised that Diamond hadn't been to see her, but she knew today was the day of the Spalding brothers' trial. Starr was certain that if Diamond hadn't been able to see her, it meant the feds were playing their paperwork game to prevent her from getting in. Her train of thought was broken by the sound of a strong tap from a metal object banging on her cell door. She was curled up, hugging her knees to conserve body heat.

"Fields! Court! Get ready! Cuff up!" the white overweight, balding guard yelled through the slot.

"Damn. Can't I at least brush my teeth?" she mumbled to herself as she stretched wide while yawning. She strolled over to the metal sink unit and used the tiny toothbrush from the intake package they had given her. The clear tube of generic toothpaste seemed to be even smaller. She quickly rinsed her mouth out and washed her face as she heard the tray slot of the steel door fall open. She ignored it as she wet her hair. She hadn't seen herself in days. But one person she couldn't wait to see was Diamond. The thought of her made Starr smile. Starr stuck her wrists out through the slot, bracing herself for what she knew was about to come.

"Agh! Bitch!" she yelled as the guard simultaneously clamped the cuffs down on both of her wrists. He smiled as he backed up and opened the cell door. Starr stepped through, squinting her eyes as she struggled to adjust to the bright lights while she was escorted to the receiving and discharge area.

Many other prisoners were being transported and processed out before they were loaded into vans. When it was time for Starr to leave, two suited federal agents were waiting up front for her. Starr recognized one of the agents immediately.

"So, we meet again," Starr sarcastically taunted Agent Costanza.

"Just shut up and keep it moving," Agent Costanza ordered.

"Don't I get to get dressed? This orange jumpsuit breeds presumption of guilt. I haven't even been formally charged with anything," Starr protested.

"Your day is coming, princess," Agent Costanza vowed with confirmation as she attempted to grab Starr's elbow. The look Starr shot her was enough to make her reconsider.

"Walk that way." She pointed straight ahead and allowed Starr to walk on her own through the sliding glass doors that led to the back exit, where the black Yukon Denali they intended to transport her in was parked. Agent Donahue was standing at the back with the passenger door wide open. Starr was ushered in and then they drove away from the Clark County Detention Center.

Chapter 16

Sparkle sat across from Glitter counting the pile of bills they had sprawled out on the living room table. Glitter was preoccupied with breaking up some of the Cali bud they had just gotten in to roll up. She had rubber-banded her sixth G stack before she paused to twist up the good-smelling weed. Things had been looking up for them ever since they'd become a part of the Double Gs family. Overnight, they had gone from mere bottle service girls in a nightclub and small-time weed pushers to forces to be reckoned with, and now they had more money and the drug they so loved than they knew what to do with. They loved what the Double Gs represented and the way they took care of their own.

Although Sparkle was excited when they had first received the news that they were chosen to join the Double Gs, in the beginning Glitter was a little skeptical about joining. She and Sparkle had been on their own since they were young teens and all they had and depended on was each other. But after becoming a Double G and getting to know members like Bubbles, who they instantly took a liking to, and a few of the other girls, Glitter was confident they had made the right choice and were where they belonged. Starr had made sure they were welcomed with open arms and she made them feel like they could take over the world. Both Glitter and Sparkle were all too prepared to rep the Double Gs for life, even if it meant putting their lives on the line.

Sparkle counted the $1,000 stacks she and Glitter had rubber-banded. "Nice," she announced. " So far, it's fourteen stacks, and we still got about another four or five to count," she added.

Glitter nodded in approval. By now, Glitter was putting fire to the blunt she had just rolled. She took a long drag of the drug. Smoke residue illuminated from her mouth and nostrils before she let out a stream of the cloud smoke. She looked down at the blunt cigar. "And this shit she gave us, some fire," Glitter stated.

They still couldn't believe Diamond had given them the bag of money for holding Bubbles down when they collected the bank robbery money from the Spalding brothers. In addition, Diamond had blessed them with a pound of California's best marijuana for their own personal use.

Glitter took another hit of the blunt then passed it to Sparkle then picked up a pile of the twenties in front of her and began counting.

Sparkle took a pull of the weed. She let the smoke hit the back of her lungs. The impact caused her to semi-gag, the way she always did whenever her and her sister had come across a batch of strong bud. "Yeah, this that fire right here!" Sparkle exclaimed through light coughs.

Glitter shook her head and smiled. She knew the drug would be too strong for her sister's weak system. Ever since they had started smoking and drinking at the young age of twelve, Sparkle's tolerance level had always been low. It was one of the main reasons why they preferred to smoke, or use any drug for that matter, in the privacy of their own home. Sparkle had a bad experience when she was sixteen. They had been chilling with some dudes and one of them slipped her a blunt laced with dust in attempt to take advantage of her. After that, they never smoked with others and never let anybody see either one of them slipping out in public.

Sparkle passed the blunt back to Glitter. Glitter stuck the blunt in her mouth as she continued counting the stack of bills. "I wasn't feelin' those Spalding mutha-fuckas," Glitter stated out of nowhere. The blunt flick-ered up and down from the tip of her lips while smoke escaped from her mouth as she spoke. "I wish that Irish bastard would've done something stupid, so I could've shown him what being a bad black bitch means!" Glitter chimed.

Sparkle laughed. "Why you gotta be a bad bitch? Why you couldn't show him how you were just a strong black woman?"

Glitter rolled her eyes at her sister. "Every time you smoke some good bud, you get on some black power shit," Glitter pointed out. "If I wanna be a bad black bitch, then that's what it is," she added. "I know I'm a strong black woman, but when I'm in the streets, I'm a bad bitch, and if a nigga test that, that's his ass!" Glitter pulled her Glock from her Ferragamo belt and kissed the side of it.

Sparkle shook her head. "Okay, bad bitch," Sparkle mocked. "I'm with you."

"You better be," Glitter told her as she passed her the blunt. Just then, Glitter's phone rang. "Wassup, B?" Glitter answered.

"Tell her I said hey," Sparkle offered. She made a waving gesture. She knew "B" was short for Bubbles.

Lately, the three of them had been hanging together. They had both been learning a lot from Bubbles about the organization as well as just about being a woman in what's considered to be a man's world. Sparkle rub-ber-banded up another G stack while Glitter sat and listened to whatever Bubbles was telling her on the other end of the phone.

"Okay, cool, we'll be ready," Glitter spoke into the phone. "And Spark says hey," Glitter added, right before the call ended.

"What's up?" Sparkle wasted no time asking.

"They locked Starr back up after they let her go," Glitter informed her sister.

"Damn, for what?" a concerned Sparkle asked.

"I dunno, but Bubbles said Diamond wants everybody to meet at Treasures," Glitter relayed.

"Okay, well, let's finish wrapping up this money then," Sparkle retorted. She passed her sister the blunt then grabbed a handful of the money and began counting.

Chapter 17

The show was on. It was time to make the grand entrance. Diamond pulled up in her Jaguar and parked in front of the courthouse. As she stepped out of the driver's side, another woman emerged from the passenger's side, walked around to the other side of the vehicle, and pulled off. Diamond ran her hands down the sides of her shapely hips and she smoothed her navy skirt. She faced the federal courthouse steps and dropped her silver leather Armani briefcase to her left side, while her right hand lowered her Gucci shades to get a clear look ahead. She then readjusted them onto the bridge of her nose and stepped from the street onto the sidewalk, prepping herself for her favorite part of the day: facing the media circus.

The courthouse's long, oval-shaped steps were filled with reporters piled on top of each other snapping photos and holding microphones and tape recorders high in the air trying to get quotes.

"No comments, no comments," Diamond politely repeated as she squeezed through the dozens of reporters who swarmed her. She upheld a vibrant smile as she soaked up all of the attention, loving every second of it. She usually showboated on the way back out. She used the opportunities to take public shots at the judicial system and hypnotize the media, leading everyone to believe it was her clients who were the actual victims, victims of injustice such as violations of amendments and constitutional rights. It was a sideshow that usually blinded those who paid any real attention, misleading them from realistic facts of incriminating evidence. O.J. Simpson's trial was the best example of such an unorthodox method. If not skillfully used right, it could end up as political suicide.

Endless questions flew Diamond's way as she slowly footed her heels up the mountain of steps. She ignored them all with her charming grin and seductive strut as her thick, shapely hips swayed from right to left. She finally made her way into the federal courthouse where the loud vanity stopped, and the quiet seriousness began. Diamond straightened up, turning on her vicious "pit bull in a skirt" frame of mind, as she set her briefcase on the X-ray machine next to the metal detector. She walked through, retrieving it on the other side.

"Hey, Sam," she greeted the longtime federal deputy who sat behind the security desk. He smiled and tipped his hat to her as she passed him. She removed her sunglasses and tucked them into her BCBG skirt suit's jacket pocket, while heading straight for the courtroom's huge burned wooden double doors.

It seemed as if all eyes were on Diamond as she entered the "arena," as she liked to call it. Only two people chose not to waste their time looking back at her, and those were the first two people she noticed. As in any courtroom, their table was positioned to the left of her table. She strutted down the long aisle and made her way to a waist-high wooden gate door that she swung open and stepped through to get to her table, where all five of her clients sat, awaiting her arrival. She didn't even acknowledge them as she set her briefcase on the table, opened it, and stood in front of it, still eyeing her opponents. She passed over the sight of Linda McCarthy and focused on Victoria Stockford. She knew little about the DA, but she'd heard how good she was. Nonetheless, Diamond knew the two of them combined was no threat. Linda was the top dog of them all. So anyone else on her team was beneath her.

The same thing that seemed to be Linda and Diamond's advantage also played to their disadvantage. They both were nothing more than mouthpieces. Both of their cases were prepared for them. They just put together the arguments. For the defense team, their law offices and paralegals did most of the research, especially of similar cases to be cited.

For the prosecution, they had the government. Everything of importance was brought to them first. They dictated the fight as far as evidence, witnesses, testimony, and jury selection. Most importantly, the DA had a personal bond with the judge. It was all pretty much laid out for them. But the challenge was making it all stick. Every move they made was contested. It all came down to how either side familiarized themselves with the personal details of the case and that's what they both did exceptionally well. It was a chess match of words. And whoever choked first would surely lose.

Chapter 18

Starr was caged in a separate holding cell, set apart from others who awaited their calendared court proceedings. She didn't mind. In fact, she preferred it that way. She had a lot of time to herself over the weekend. It gave her a clear chance to think, and mentally sort situations out. Things that seemed to be out of order were put back into perspective. Retrospect and hindsight were reviewed with thorough recollection. The entire past was reevaluated, the present was updated, and the future was calculated.

Her peaceful moment was interrupted by Agent Costanza's shadow appearing in her dimly lit cell. Starr looked up and saw her newest rival.

"Here!" Agent Costanza yelled, holding up a bag.

Starr stood up and snatched it from her. She smiled to herself, thinking of Diamond. She knew that's where the clothes had come from. She watched the shadow on the back wall disappear and then she got dressed.

Once her new attire was on, she felt like a new woman. The clothes fit Starr perfectly. She figured that as sexually intimate as they were, Diamond knew her body so well. She stripped out of the orange jumpsuit and squeezed into the snug, curve-gripping all-black Donna Karan jeans, and then slipped the white satin short-sleeved blouse over her head. The bottom of it fell perfectly at her waistline. She then stepped into the white pair of ankle-high multi-strap heels. She went over to the sink unit and wet her hair, slicking it back behind her ears. She sat back down on the cold, hard bench and crossed her legs.

Within a matter of minutes, footsteps could be heard approaching, along with the distinct sound of handcuffs, clicking as if whoever had them played with them like some sort of toy. Two shadows reached the cell before their bodies. This time, both Agent Costanza and her partner approached the cell bars.

"Cuff up. It's your turn," Agent Costanza.

"I haven't met with my lawyer yet," Starr retorted.

Agent Costanza impatiently grew frustrated. She released a sigh to show it as she shifted the weight of her body to her left foot. "Honey, please. This is a bail hearing, not your long-awaited sentencing. Don't rush the clock. You'll cheat death that way and, by doing that, you'd be cheating us all."

Starr rolled her eyes. She was getting sick of Agent Costanza's puny, pale-face self. Unbeknownst to her, she was quickly climbing to the top of Starr's hit list. Starr stood up and walked to the bars, stuck her wrists through, and was cuffed before she was escorted down the hall. She was led through a single large wooden door, and into the front side of a huge courtroom, which she studied every inch of as she was ushered to the table on her right side. On her way over she looked to the back of the courtroom. The wooden benches were packed with many viewers, even some media. Starr quickly singled out Monica's smile. It was the only friendly face in the crowd. Everyone else looked overwhelmed, confused, or impatient.

Her evaluation was cut short by her approaching the empty table, where two chairs sat. She wasn't allowed to be seated yet. The agents stood behind her like Al-Qaeda was about to rush in at any moment and shoot up the courtroom in a daring attempt to free her. She ignored them and focused on what was in front of her.

There were two men who had approached the high wooden wall of the judge's bench. Judge Saber was an elderly white man with pure white hair. He was looking down on the two men as the three of them whispered in discussion. The judge kept his left hand over the microphone to protect their dialogue from being overheard. The man on the right swiftly turned to catch brief eye contact with Starr and then he jumped back into his hushed conversation. Starr frowned at his cheap polyester suit.

The rest of the courtroom was quiet. Starr allowed her mind to drift again as she waited for Diamond to make her famous grand entrance through the double doors in the back. She took another quick glance behind her, looked back at the doors and then at Monica, who seemed to be closer than before. She thought she could smell Monica's familiar scent as they held their gazes for a fair amount of seconds. An image of their encounter in her office invaded Starr's thoughts.

The brief thought was interrupted by Agent Costanza's spiteful move to purposely stand in Starr's way to obstruct her view. Both agents remained professionally militant, much like the guards who stood outside of Buckingham Palace. Starr was tempted to shove Agent Costanza but she knew it would only make matters worse.

Starr's thoughts were interrupted by the man in the cheap suit walking over to her table. Surprisingly, he stood next to her and the agents stepped back. The other man in the much more expensive suit went over to the table on the left. The judge looked down at his notes as someone announced the next case on the docket sheet. Starr missed whose voice it was and almost foolishly blamed the elderly female stenographer who was typing every word down. It was like a blind person typing Braille notes.

"The United States versus Starrshma Fields," the female voice continued.

The entire United States? Versus me? I'm honored, Starr joked to herself. *And who is this stupid-looking man?*

"I'm Lionel Osborne," he whispered to her, reading her mind. "Ms. Morgan has a big trial going on downstairs that she couldn't break away from. She said you would understand and to tell you she'll see you later." The lawyer gave Starr a wink. Starr just shook her head.

The judge reviewed the bail package as the DA began to speak in the most elegant and professional manner. "Your Honor, allow me to express to the court that Ms. Fields is a guaranteed flight risk whose sources are unlimited. I am quite confident that she is willing to make any bail set by the court today and is just as eagerly willing to leave it behind as a donation; we will never see her again."

Public Defender Osborne intervened. "Need I remind this court that Ms. Felps—"

"Fields," the DA humorously corrected with a self-pleasing smile.

Starr shot Osborne a look of disgust.

Osborne was embarrassed. "'Scuse me. Ms. Fields," he corrected himself, "hasn't even been indicted on the charges. She's being held on a criminal complaint, for God's sake! She should be ROR. Better yet, she shouldn't even be here in the first place. I can say this: if she posts bail, even the highest set by the court, it's only because she plans on returning for the money and the property put up. She has three signatories ready to put their wealth on the line and be held responsible for her returning to court. These people are all taxpaying, law-abiding pillars of their community. Ms. Fields has no prior record; she's only been arrested once, but was fully acquitted of all charges. There isn't any reason bail should be—"

Before the public defender finished his last remark he was cut short. "Denied!" Judge Saber yelled as he smacked the wooden gavel into the desk. "Rehearing in two weeks. Next case."

Starr couldn't believe her ears.

Monica watched as Starr was shoved back out of the courtroom. She waited until the door closed behind Starr and the agents. She smiled. Then she got up and exited the courtroom.

Chapter 19

As far back as she could remember, Diamond always wanted to be a lawyer. It was in her blood. Her mother was a prestigious lawyer, her father owned a private law firm, and his father was a judge, most famous for dying on the bench after catching a heart attack while sentencing a convicted murderer to a double life sentence. When it was time for the murderer to speak, ironically he told Judge Rugby Morgan to "Go to hell." The story quickly became a legend, and a myth, for decades after, and still circulated, mostly from those just finishing law school. It seemed to be a real conversation icebreaker. "Hey, did you hear about . . ." And it would be all downhill from there.

For Diamond, her position had not come as hard-earned as she would have liked. People always tried to hand her what she would rather much work for. The people in high places she knew weren't an advantage for her. They were a handicap. They weakened her respect. At times, she was close to changing her last name just to get a fair chance of not being favored before even meeting the people she had to go through to get to the top. As hard as she tried to shake it, her family name still shaped who she was today. Her becoming a Double Gs member was just an act of rebellion. She figured that if she was going to possess so much unearned power, she wanted it to be from her own will, position, and actions. That's the opportunity that being an elite Double Gs member gave her.

It all started from when she was young. As an only child, Diamond was very sheltered by her parents. She went to the best all-girls private schools from kindergarten to college. Being that her parents were always drowned in their work, stacks of files would be all over their huge house. When Diamond was old enough to read them, when her parents weren't looking she would study the private lives of the thousands of criminals who came through her upper-class community home's front door in paper form.

It became obsessively addictive. She did away with the regular novels such as Anne Rice's infamous murder mysteries, and the TV shows like *CSI, Law & Order,* and many other forms of investigative entertainment. This was a new reality she had gotten a hold of. She would read her mother's handwritten notes about the cases. She would agree with most, and differ with others. The strangest part about that was that every detail she used to disagree with were the same ones that her mother would come home talking to her father about, revealing that those were the reasons she lost the case, never knowing Diamond was paying attention. Over the years, Diamond realized that her mother was brilliantly textbook smart, but close-minded. Elizabeth Morgan was a high-profile lawyer, but in the most basic form.

Elizabeth Morgan was the best at proving innocence, factual innocence. But most of her clients were really guilty. She lacked the toughness to place herself in the criminal's shoes and think like one. She didn't verbally manipulate the facts to her advantage. She left the DA she went up against daily unchallenged; and most of the cases she did win with a guilty client were because of the family's name.

Diamond wanted to be different. She had come across so many of the same cases with similar details; she had memorized the pattern of recidivism. Within seconds of meeting a client, she could instantly tell if they were guilty and actually be accurate in her conclusion. And that's exactly how she would greet them as she approached the situation. "Hi. You're guilty. Let's see what we can do about that." With such a bold and honest tactic, the criminals felt more comfortable not holding back from her. They would walk her through the crimes scene by scene as she would listen, take notes, and ask specific questions as to why they didn't choose a better method. She would even go further by making suggestions of what they should've done differently to not get caught or be suspected.

During Diamond's semesters off from Howard University, where she majored in criminal justice, she would work in her father's law firm as a paralegal. It provided excellent hands-on experience for her. She made it her business to gain personal knowledge about every case that was being worked on. Some of the other employees were annoyed by her probing, and others would welcome her with positive encouragement. She gravitated to it all.

One day, the newest case had just come in. Everyone was so busy that no one really paid it much attention just yet. It seemed pretty much open and shut. So when Brenda McMillan adopted the case as her own, it was just for the quick paycheck. She had no intention of fighting for the defendant. For what? A young college girl home on spring break got pulled over in a stolen car, with a stolen gun under the seat, which turned out to be the first murder weapon of multiple homicides a few years back. Brenda's plan was to get the girl the best deal possible and force her to cop out to a negotiated plea bargain. Case closed. Check cleared.

Diamond had discovered the file accidentally. She had gone out for coffee and brought Brenda back a cup of her favorite Starbucks flavor, French vanilla.

Brenda had stepped out, so Diamond set the cup on her desk, right next to the folder with the mug shot of one of the most beautiful young girls she had ever seen. The name, vertically, went up the folder's right-hand corner: STARRSHMA FIELDS. Out of pure interest, Diamond set her own cup of coffee down as she sat in Brenda's seat and opened up the file. From the beginning, nothing seemed to be adding up.

Brenda returned from her smoke break, strolling to her desk, savoring the nicotine rush she got from the two Marlboro Lights she had just chain-smoked. She wasn't at all surprised to see Diamond sitting at her desk in her seat. She smiled down at the young protégé and sat on the edge of her desk. Brenda was a redheaded white woman in her early forties.

"And what are you up to, young lady?" Brenda asked, smelling like a cloud of smoke.

Diamond shook her head from side to side, staring in the folder, flipping pages without ever looking up at Brenda. "This isn't right. It doesn't make any sense. None of it. I want this case. I want this to be my first solo. You can get the credit, and the check." She finally looked up at Brenda and stared her in her blue eyes. "I want this one." It was evident that she wasn't taking no for an answer.

First, Diamond had to track down twenty-one-year-old Starr, who had managed to make a $750,000 bail the day after her arrest. Starr had hardly even gotten the chance to see a holding cell. It was apparent that someone in a very high place was on her side. That was a major point that intrigued Diamond. She found out that Starr was allowed to leave town to go back to school, but she had to report to a pre-trial probation officer once a week. A signed copy of their agreement was on file. Starr's cellular number was listed. *Diamond called her up and arranged for them to meet back in New York.*

During that time Starr and Diamond became very close. Starr physically walked Diamond through everything that had happened, and exactly where it all took place. She was totally truthful with Diamond but insisted on withholding one thing: why she did it. At the time, she couldn't reveal such highly classified information. Eventually, Diamond would come to know everything.

Diamond was aggressive with Starr's case. She attacked it day and night. She was thoroughly convinced that there wasn't any way that the case should even make it to trial. On the day that Starr had been indicted by the grand jury, Diamond put in a motion for suppression of all evidence. If they won that, all charges would be dropped because they wouldn't even have a case. Diamond was confident that she could pull it off, and her chance finally came.

Although Brenda McMillan sat at the defense table, she didn't play a single part in the entire case. She was only present for show. Diamond hadn't passed the bar exam yet, but was still permitted to cross-examine the DA's witnesses, and verbally contest the evidence. Brenda didn't care. The check had gotten larger than she had ever expected. And it came along with a free show.

As a smokescreen to drag out the entire process, the expert testimony was always first. There was no jury, only a judge who had to rely on the facts presented. The first expert was a representative of the gun company that manufactured the Glock 9. His testimony was pointless. Diamond felt no need to cross-examine him or any of the others who weren't actual witnesses to the crime scene. In fact, there were only two: the hotel maid

*and the arresting officer. The maid was called first by
the district attorney. The middle-aged Hispanic maid
was introduced and sworn in.*

Diamond remembered it well. *The DA began to ask his
questions.* "Ms. Gonzalez, on the night in question you
called the police, correct?"

"Correct," *she answered in a low tone, staring into her
lap.*

Diamond noticed that Selena Gonzalez was dressed
in her maid uniform. *It was no doubt a beautiful tactic
by the DA to make her look more like a credible witness
than she actually was. Textbook.*

"What caused you to do so?" *DA Redman asked.*

"As I was coming down the hall to make my rounds, I
heard screaming." *Her Dominican accent thickened.*

"Screaming?"

"Yes, screaming."

"Like, yelling? Shouting?"

"No. Like pain or torture."

"Humph. Really?" *The DA placed his fist under his chin
and let it all sink in before he continued.* "And what did
you do?"

"Well, I was scared at first. I didn't know which room
it was coming from, but I was sure someone was in distress. So I turned back around and went downstairs to
use the emergency phone. I reported what I heard and
then ran back up to the third floor, which was where I
heard the screaming. As I looked down the hall, I saw
a woman exiting one of the rooms on the far end in a
hurry. She ran right toward me and passed me by. She
looked as if she had done something terribly wrong, so
I ran downstairs after her, but she left through the back
door into the parking lot, so I went back to the phone
and called the police again."

"And is that woman in here today?"

"Yes," she confirmed.

"Can you be so kind as to point her out?"

She nervously pointed directly at Starr.

"Let the record show the witness pointed out the defendant. And then what happened next?" he asked as he turned his attention back to the maid.

"Well, the police instructed me to stay put, but I ran back upstairs to see what happened. I was too late. I walked back down the hall and saw one of the doors was halfway open. It appeared to be the same room the woman came out of. I walked in and saw a bed full of blood-soaked sheets. That's when I called the police again."

"And no one else was there?"

"There had to be, but not when I got there."

The DA looked up at the judge. "No further questions, Your Honor."

The judge looked down at Diamond. "Ms. Morgan, your witness."

Diamond had been taking notes during the entire testimony. Not acknowledging the judge, she waited to finish what she was writing before she got up and approached the witness stand, smiling.

"Hello, Ms. Gonzalez. How are you?"

"I'm fine," the maid replied with a shaky voice.

"Okay. Well, I'm going to make this real quick and simple because you've been such a huge help to this case already." Everyone's eyebrows rose from Diamond's comment. "Okay, so a few things. Now, you said that you heard screaming?"

"Yes."

"Was it loud?"

"Very."

"What time was this about?"

"Three-fifteen a.m."

"Now, this is where I need you to be very clear. Could you distinguish what sex the person's voice was?"

"I believe it was a man."

"A man? Deep voice?"

"Kind of."

"Okay then. Let's just say a man was screaming. Have you ever heard any types of noises coming from any of the other hotel rooms since you've been working there?"

The maid blushed. "Well, it is a hotel, so . . . yes."

"What kind?"

"Umm, arguing, fighting, and partying, but mostly sex."

"Hmm. Mostly sex. Could it have been possible that those were, in fact, screams of passion?"

"Umm. Maybe, but I doubt it. He was very much in pain."

"Are you some kind of expert on pain and sex?"

The woman was stunned as much as she was caught off guard. "No. Not really."

"So how can you determine which was which?"

She was baffled. The DA tried to jump in and save her. "Objection! This isn't going anywhere!"

"I'm trying to establish whether the authorities should've even been called in the first place, since that's what led to my client's arrest."

"I'll allow it. Proceed, but get to the point, Ms. Morgan," the judge grumbled.

"Thank you, Your Honor. Okay, moving along. You pointed out my client, did you not?"

"Yes. I did."

"Yes. You did. But you stated that you left the floor after hearing the screams, you called the police, and then you returned to the floor, where you saw my client coming from an unspecified room. Other than that, she just ran past you. Your personal opinion was that she was guilty of something. What was she wearing?"

"*Umm. A black silk minidress, with black heels.*"

"*And she ran past you in heels?*"

"*Yes.*"

"*So, she could've been just as scared as you. Maybe she was going to call for help like you did. She may have even been the victim.*"

"*It didn't seem that way at the time.*"

"*At the time,*" Diamond mocked. "*And you chased after her?*"

"*Yes.*"

"*Why?*"

"*I believed she had done something wrong.*"

"*Is that the procedure the hotel trained you to use in the event of a suspected violent crime?*"

"*No.*"

"*So, if you felt someone was in distress, why wouldn't you choose to help them instead of trying to be a hero?*"

"*Objection!*" the DA yelled.

"*Sustained. Watch it, Ms. Morgan.*"

"*Will do, Your Honor. Okay, so you heard something when you left the first time. But when you returned there was no screaming. Just a woman running. You left again, and then returned to the floor, went to a room where you felt like a crime had been committed, but you found no victim. No signs of any real crime other than the sheets with barely any blood on it.*" Diamond spun around and faced the judge. "*Let the record show Exhibit A. No further questions,*" Diamond declared. Pictures of the bloodstained sheets were passed to the judge by the bailiff.

The DA had been itching to call his ace in the hole. "*I now call to the stand Officer Stockbridge.*"

A white uniformed officer in his mid-twenties approached the bench and was sworn in. The DA got right to it. "*Could you describe, in your own words or those of your report, what happened on the night of which we speak?"*

"Yes. Ahem." Officer Stockbridge cleared his throat by lightly coughing into his closed right fist. "I was responding to a disturbance call, which was probably the result of a physical assault of some kind."

"And what was the location?"

"The Super 8 off of the Freemont Street area."

"And can you describe what happened as you approached the scene?"

"Well, from afar, I saw a young woman dash to a vehicle, and I saw the maid who just testified running out of the building, chasing her."

"And what did you do?"

"I saw the fleeing woman run to a vehicle past me. I made a U-turn and followed it for a few miles and then I pulled her over."

"And was the woman acting suspicious as if she had anything to hide?"

"Certainly."

"So then what happened?"

"I asked her to step out of the vehicle. I cuffed her, placed her in the back of the squad car, and I searched the vehicle."

"And what did you find?"

"A gun. Under the driver's seat."

"A gun! Under the seat. Wow. Totally accessible. And upon further investigation, what were the findings?"

"Well, for one, the vehicle was stolen. For two, the weapon was stolen. And later in the week the ballistics came back that matched two homicides."

"Wow. Two murders. And what did the suspect in custody have to say about all of this?"

"She claimed to not know anything."

"And is she here in this very courtroom today?"

"Yes, sir. Right there."

"Let the record show that, yet again, Ms. Fields was pointed out. Thank you very much, Officer Stockbridge. You've done a fine job." The DA walked back to his table, sat in his seat, and tasted the sweetness of victory.

"Ms. Morgan, you may cross-examine," the judge declared.

Once again, Diamond had been jotting down notes and didn't react or respond until she was finished. She then got up, not smiling this time, and stormed to the witness stand in full attack mode.

"Officer Stockbridge, how long have you been on the force?" She spoke with unwavering, passionate aggression.

"A little over a year and a half, ma'am."

"Ms. Morgan will do just fine," she corrected him. "And in that little over a year and a half," she mocked, "have you ever made any routine traffic arrests?"

"Quite a few. Yes."

"Oh!" Diamond retorted as if she was surprised. "So you are familiar with the proper procedures then. Aren't you?" she sarcastically asked as if she didn't know at first.

"Yes. Yes, I am."

"Okay. So let's just get into it. You saw my client getting into a vehicle, at a speed that you didn't agree with, and instead of checking up on the initial dispatched call you left the original crime scene. But first, let's get this clear. The call said nothing about a woman running to a car, correct?"

Officer Stockbridge began to look uneasy. "No," he replied with a cracked voice.

"No," she repeated. "So then what did you do?"

"Well, I called for backup and I went after the suspicious vehicle."

"Oh. So now the vehicle was suspicious as well. Was it speeding?"

"Umm, not really, but—"

"Were any traffic laws broken?" Diamond interrupted.

"Not exactly, but—"

"Did you run the plates?"

"Yes, I ran the plates."

"And what came up?"

"It was a black Lexus LS 450, with tinted windows, registered to a Hubert Wallace."

"Oh, so it wasn't stolen?"

"No. Not at the time, but—"

"No. I repeat, it wasn't stolen, it wasn't speeding, it didn't run any red lights, or in fact do anything else wrong, for that matter. A woman was simply leaving the hotel. So, you pulled my client over. What did she do?"

"She stopped."

"Just like that? Nothing to hide? She just stopped."

"Objection!" the DA yelled.

"Overruled. Continue, Ms. Morgan. Just watch it."

"Yes, sir, Your Honor. Okay, so, you walked up to the vehicle, and . . ."

"And I asked for her documents. She appeared nervous and was acting suspicious."

"Yet, she still complied," she stated more than asked.

"Yes."

"And did it all check out?"

"Yes. Well, she didn't physically have her driver's license on her, but she did provide a college ID. I ran her name and everything checked out. She didn't know where the vehicle's documents were, such as the registration and insurance, so she searched around. I knew something was wrong."

"Sure. I'm certain you did," she teased. "But, none-theless, she found them and provided them with no resistance. I imagine that a screwdriver with a gang bandana covering it was sticking out of the steering wheel? Wait, no. I believe the official report states that the car was hot-wired, wasn't it?"

"Objection!" the DA screamed at the top of his lungs.

The judge looked down at Officer Stockbridge. "You may answer the question."

Officer Stockbridge began sweating profusely. He desperately wanted to remove his hat and loosen his tie. He was frying in his uniform. "No, ma'am. I . . . I mean, Ms. Morgan. The keys were in the ignition."

"Wow. The keys were in it and yet you still pulled her out of the vehicle, frisked her, which is the job for a female officer, you cuffed her, and you put her in the squad car like some guilty criminal."

"I . . . I asked her for permission to search." The officer stumbled over his words.

"And as an honest, college-attending, taxpaying citizen, whose precious time you were wasting, she complied to make your job easier. Did she give you permission to detain her?"

"Uh, no, but—"

"So there's a chance that she may not have agreed to the search if she would've known she'd be criminally detained."

"I can't say."

"Well, I'm sure she'll clear it up for us if she has to take the stand, which she may do," Diamond announced while turning to stare the DA in the eyes as it sank in. She then cracked a slight smile and faced Officer Stockbridge again. "But I'm sure it won't have to come to that," she proclaimed. She then looked back at Starr and winked. Starr smiled. Brenda was thoroughly impressed.

"So, Officer Stockbridge, did you physically search my client?"

Officer Stockbridge choked as he looked over at the DA's blood-flushed face. The DA looked away as if Officer Stockbridge was on his own. "Uh, yes, but only to—"

"It's on the record that my client was a provocatively dressed young woman. You physically ran your hands up and down her body?"

"Uh, for safety reasons I—"

"Why didn't you call for female backup? Isn't that the correct procedure?"

"Under normal circum—"

"And these were considered extreme circumstances?" she asked before he could finish his response. "No! This sounds more like a sexual harassment civil suit to me!"

"Objection, Your Honor!" the DA yelled as he smacked his open palms down on the table and jumped to his feet.

"Sustained. I warned you, Ms. Morgan. Next time you will be ejected," the judge threatened.

Diamond smiled and ignored him. She didn't plan on being much longer anyway. "So, again, what did you find?"

"A pistol under the seat," he proudly stated.

"That's all?" Diamond downplayed.

"Yes."

"Did you question my client about it?"

"She says she didn't know it was there, or that it was in her car."

"But of course. You knew it wasn't her vehicle. And yet, even further, that gun was linked to two different homicides, on two different occasions. Years apart. But she still allowed you to find it so easily."

Officer Stockbridge didn't know how to respond. "Correct." That was all that he could come up with.

Diamond's point was silently made. "Okay, moving along, let's get to the crimes she was eventually charged with. The vehicle wasn't reported stolen until about an hour later, correct?"

"Umm, yes."

"So at the time, she was a legitimate driver."

Officer Stockbridge looked to the DA for help. The DA's eyes shot up at the ceiling. *"Yes,"* he nervously answered.

"And this gun—I have the ballistic reports here—my client's fingerprints aren't anywhere on it. But there are fingerprints on it, proving she didn't wipe it down. Did you find any gloves of any sort lying around?"

"No."

"So it was impossible for my client to have handled this weapon. At least up until the most recent events, correct?"

"Maybe." Officer Stockbridge shifted in his seat. *"It would seem so,"* he agreed, wiping his dry mouth with his sweaty palm.

"Now, let's talk about the murders traced back to the gun. See, my client is only twenty-one years old. One of the murdered victims was a known drug dealer who was found dead three years ago. My client was eighteen years old then, a straight A student in her last year of high school. The next victim was another well-known thief who robbed local drug dealers. That murder took place last year. My client was away in college, in another state."

The DA jumped up, not wanting to hear another word. *"Your Honor, the prosecution motions to dismiss all charges."*

Becoming a federal attorney was the best thing Diamond had ever felt she had done. After more than nine years, she had finally made her own lane, where now, when the Morgan last name came into play, people expressed fear of her first name. As if they would rather go up against anyone else but her.

Diamond sat next to her clients, waiting for Judge Catero to exit her chambers. Diamond looked over at McCarthy and another agent whispering in each other's ears as they reviewed their notes. Everyone's attention was ripped apart.

"All rise!" The Honorable Nancy Catero approached the bench and put on her reading glasses before sitting down. Everyone else stood tall as she did. Diamond could hardly contain her smile, knowing that the curtain was about to rise and the show was about to begin, starting with her favorite opening: jury selection. Diamond thought back to her years as an undergrad.

"May the best woman win!" Those famous words were spoken by her roommate, Georgiana, as they stood side by side in the mirror, checking their makeup one final time before heading to the club. She was dressed like the cheap slut Diamond figured her out to be. Her leopard-print cat suit left nothing to the imagination.

Georgiana ran her fingers through her short, spiked hair, while Diamond tossed her long braids about, leaving a few dangling in her face. Puckering her full lips, Georgiana took out her black lipstick and went over her lips again. Diamond refreshed hers with cherry lip gloss, and it was popping!

Unlike the queen of sluts, she was dressed a bit more conservatively in a pink and black pinstriped bustier and a sleek pair of black pants, along with the perfect pair of stilettos. She readjusted the twins and exposed a bit more cleavage. I got to show a little something if I'm competing with Georgiana. Why she wasted her weekends prowling and competing with Georgiana was a mystery to her, but she did it anyway.

Georgiana's inner whore was always visible, and she had no shame in her game. At first, Diamond thought it was cute because she started college on the rebound, look-ing for hard, swollen clits and harder hearts. Diamond wasn't trying to fall in love with nobody else after the whammy her ex put on her. She was down with the "wham bam thank you, ma'am." Georgiana added more spice and upped the ante to their pussy prowling by sug-gesting that they compete. She ended up "winning" most of the time because, after talking to some of the women, Diamond wouldn't have fucked them anyway! Tonight was different, though; at least, it was for Diamond. She and Georgiana were going after the sexy DJ T-Skillz, and she would be damned if Georgiana added her sexy, thick ass as another notch on her belt. Something about T-Skillz told Diamond that she was looking for love, not just a good lay.

Their decision to target T-Skillz was made last week-end while they ate at the Italian Grill. They always got a bite to eat before going to the club.

"I wonder if that sexy DJ will be there, tonight," Georgiana had said, more to herself than Diamond.

"What about the bitch you brought home just last night?" she asked Georgiana. This girl changed bitches and niggas like decent bitches changed muthafuckin' drawers! But T-Skillz was off-limits! "I have kinda had my eye on T for a minute." Diamond gave Georgiana a stern look and continued, "So don't even try it."

Rolling her eyes, Georgiana picked up the menu and said, "Ooh, this chicken parmesan looks really good with the fettuccini pasta. What are you having, a salad?" Georgiana smirked. Of course, she was hinting at Diamond's weight. Georgiana knew that Diamond was insecure about the weight she had packed on her fresh-man year of college. Georgiana figured that it was the reason her ex-girlfriend cheated on her with anyone she encountered. Georgiana wasn't worried about T-Skillz choosing Diamond over her, but Di was determined to prove her wrong.

After they placed their orders, Georgiana brought the subject of T back up. "You do know that T is a single woman, right?" she asked coyly.

"And your point is?" Diamond challenged.

She leaned across the table and whispered, "Game on, bitch. We both want her, so let's see who she wants."

Diamond laughed. "You better bring your A game, Georgie, because something tells me T is about more than the panties."

"Oh, yeah? Well, something tells me she'll choose my panties and keep thirsting for more."

Diamond extended her right hand across the table, and they shook on it. "It's on!"

Determined to be the sexiest woman at Club Curves to get T-Skillz' affection, she raced over to Frederick's of Hollywood after class the following Friday. There she found the perfect pink and black pinstriped bustier to match her satin black pants; and then she went to Nine West and found the perfect matching stiletto sandals. Then she treated herself to a manicure and pedicure, complete with pink and black French-tipped nails. Diamond's microbraids were still fresh, so she wasn't worried about her hair.

As they headed out of the apartment that fateful Friday night, Georgiana suggested that they take Diamond's car. "After all, you'll need a ride home tonight. I'll be with T."

"Oh, that's fine by me. I don't mind you driving my car; that's if you can handle a stick," Diamond replied, her silky voice dripping with sarcasm. They argued back and forth as the young women raced toward Club Curves in the midnight blue Honda Accord. If I had an eject button for the passenger seat, her trifling behind would be soaring through the air praying she lands at the club, *Diamond thought.*

DJ T-Skillz's sexy face and hypnotizing eyes were the first things Diamond saw when they entered Club Curves. She couldn't stop looking at her and imagining what she would look like naked. There was something so familiar about the woman. Diamond couldn't put her finger on it, but she was ready to put every inch of her body on T's body. The toys made her pussy feel good, but she was ready to be held. Even the Magic Wand massager couldn't do that.

Georgiana left Diamond by herself as soon as they walked in. Somebody came by and meowed at her cat suit. She followed him to the bar for a drink then out to the dance floor. That was one reason why Diamond didn't like clubbing with Georgiana. She was often left sitting alone at a table. Tonight would be different, though. Diamond was going to have some fun. She had decided to have a good time, even if no one asked her to dance. Besides, they were supposed to be there for T.

After downing a Sex on the Beach, she had the nerve to dance alone. Diamond noticed T watching her as she strutted to the dance floor. She set her equipment on auto-selection, playing nothing but the hottest songs, some that reminded her of her high school years. "Ooh, this was my jam!" Diamond yelled as she worked her hips to "Want It, Need It" by Plies and Ashanti.

Georgiana danced over to her, and said, "You know she's playing that sexy jam for me."

Diamond rolled her eyes at her ignorant roommate. "Whatever!" She swore she had it going on.

Georgiana was ready to let Diamond know that once she set her sights on someone, no woman, not even her, could steal them away. But little did Georgiana know that this wasn't just any ordinary night, and T wasn't any ordinary woman. Georgiana worked her slim hips and big butt, rubbing her hands all over her body. She had her eyes fixed on T. T-Skillz stared at her, shaking her head as though she felt sorry for her.

Diamond wanted to laugh out loud because she looked ridiculous. Georgiana looked like a porn star on crack in the middle of a seizure! There she was, in a crowded club making love to herself, while women and even some men looked on in disgust. But Georgiana didn't care. She squeezed her breasts together while biting down on her bottom lip. She traced her lips with her tongue, while rubbing her hands between her thighs and touching her clit. T was watching all right, but she was watching Diamond dance to the beat!

T-Skillz manually selected Jahiem's "Anything." She turned it on low volume and began to speak. "Y'all listen up! This poem is dedicated to the most beautiful woman in the house!" Then she proceeded to recite a poem about passion and desire.

After her poem, she walked her way over to where Diamond was. "Hey, beautiful," T said, approaching them.

"Hey, yourself," Georgiana answered. "Thanks for the poem, babe. It was beautiful. I've been feeling you for a while. I'm glad that tonight is our night," she said, trying to sound seductive as she pressed her body against T's.

"Ma, that poem wasn't for you." Georgiana was really feeling herself way too much. T's words brought that stuck-up hussy down a notch, and her face crumbled. "It was for Diamond," she continued. Walking away, T pointed toward the floor. "You should pick that up."

"What?" Georgiana asked as she searched the dirty floor.

"Your face! You're feeling yourself way too much, Georgiana."

The whole club couldn't help but laugh as Georgiana huffed, puffed, and stormed off with some guy. Georgiana figured that would make T-Skillz jealous. Puh-leeze!

"Hi, T," *Diamond finally replied, smiling from ear to ear.*

"Diamond, I have been trying to get up the nerve to talk to you since high school."

"That's funny; I don't remember you from high school," *she told her.* Maybe that's why she looks so familiar to me. *But still, Diamond didn't remember. Besides, if she had known her then, she could have avoided her terrible relationship with her ex, Sherrell.* "I wish I had known you in high school. I'd have never wasted my time with that ho, Sherrell."

T-Skillz looked deep into her eyes and said, "Baby, it's okay. We all have to find our own paths and our own way before anything real can ever come into our lives." *That made Diamond smile brighter than ever, just for her.*

"Diamond, I was hoping that you would come back to the club. I wrote that poem for you."

She couldn't deny that she was impressed that she'd taken the time to write a poem just for her. "So just what was it that you were trying to say?" *Diamond flirtatiously inquired.*

T's face grew serious as she said, "What I'm saying is that I wanna get next to you, and not just for one night."

Just as she opened her mouth to ask Diamond to dance, Georgiana walked up to them with a disgusted look on her face. Her simpleton self obviously didn't get the message the first time. She had to come back and get embarrassed twice.

"T, why you frontin' like you want Diamond's fat ass? Is this a joke or somethin'? You know I'm the fine one. You know you want this," *the jealous bitch said while pointing between her funky legs*. This slut ain't but a Happy Meal from being a big girl her damn self, and she got the nerve to talk. *She was two seconds from Diamond fucking her all the way up and then backhanding her across the room!*

"Naw, Georgiana; you just don't get it, do you? I don't want you. You not even a little bit sexy to me! You are way too thin for me. There's nothing you can ever do for me except stay off clit and my strap-on!" T once again turned back to Diamond. "Dance with me, boo. Please?"

Georgiana couldn't believe her ears! A fine-ass woman was choosing Diamond over her.

She chuckled and said, "Okay." *The look on Georgiana's face was priceless! That would teach her to sneak in those damn big girl jokes!*

Diamond leaned forward and whispered in T-Skillz's ear, "Hold me tight."

"Only if I never have to let you go," *was her reply as she grabbed her and pulled her close. It felt so good to be in her arms. She wanted T to hold her like that forever.*

At the end of the night T asked, "Did you drive or ride with Georgiana?" *It was after two in the morning, and her DJ equipment was being packed up.*

"I drove my car."

Georgiana had long since left the club with some nigga named Jerrell. After getting dissed by T, they guessed she was still determined to have somebody between her legs for the night.

"Would you like to get a bite to eat at the Pancake House?" *she offered.*

"That's cool, or maybe I could just make us breakfast back at my place." *It wasn't Diamond's intention to sleep with her, at least not that night, but she did want her all to herself and not in a crowded restaurant with a bunch of afterhours clubbers.*

Her lips turned upward in a smile as she replied, "Only if you promise to respect me in the morning!"

She packed the last of her equipment into her SUV and followed Diamond back to her place, where T-Skillz made her breakfast as they could hear Georgiana entertaining.

"Shit! Damn! Shit! Oooooh!" Georgiana was yelling as her long acrylic nails scratched down the panel wall. Apparently, her scrub from the club was hitting her spot.

"Is she always this easy?" T, better known as Tina, asked. Diamond simply answered with an affirmative nod.

"I don't understand a woman who doesn't know her worth," she commented as she scooped up eggs with her fork and packed them into her sexy mouth, devouring them in a few chews.

After breakfast, they went to Diamond's bedroom to watch movies. Tina noticed her high school yearbook, picked it up, and thumbed through the pages. "You really don't remember me from school, do you?" she asked.

"I'm afraid I don't."

"Atinia Sampson doesn't ring a bell?" She held up the book and motioned for Diamond to look at one of the pictures. When she sat next to her, she pointed at a tall, slinky tomboy in the back of the class photo and said, "That's me."

It was then and only then that Diamond remembered Tina from biology class. She had been the smartest in the class. Long gone were her broken eyeglasses held together by duct tape. She now sported contacts. Her huge, outdated hairstyle had been replaced by soft, silky curls. She had also given up the high-water pants and T-shirts. Standing at a thick and sexy six feet, Atinia Sampson now possessed sex appeal that no one ever

thought she would have had back in school! No wonder I
didn't remember her from school. Wow.

*While watching movies, Tina and Diamond fell asleep
in each other's arms, but they were awakened by the
noises coming from Georgiana's room. Diamond closed
her eyes tight and pulled the covers over her head. But
not even that drowned out the noise coming from the
other side of the thin wall. Georgiana was still getting
her back banged out by her latest conquest. The fool
looked a little young for Georgiana, who was in her
damn mid-twenties. But based on the sounds Georgiana
was making, he must have been all man! He had her
screaming and climbing the fucking wall! She was
pounding on the wall, as if she was submitting to his
every wish. There was no way Tina and Diamond could
sleep until their session was over.*

*Frustrated and exhausted, Diamond pounded on
the wall. Several minutes later, the noises ended with
Georgiana's young companion grunting like a wounded
animal, and Georgiana squealing like a stuck pig. It
was easy to guess that they had both peaked. They were
just as happy about it as Georgiana and ol' boy were.
Tina and Diamond looked at each other and let out sighs
of relief that they could finally get some sleep.*

*At least, that's what they thought. It wasn't ten minutes
later that they heard the bed rocking again! Diamond
pulled her pillow over her face and tried to drown the
noises out, once again. Tina laughed and wrapped her
arms around her.*

*The next morning when she stumbled into the kitchen,
Georgiana was already up.* "Good morning!" *she sang.*

"For whom?" *Diamond rolled her eyes while downing
a cup of black coffee. She'd only managed three hours of
sleep thanks to Georgiana's sexual marathon.*

Georgiana laughed. "I'm sorry, Diamond." *Again, she
rolled her eyes. Georgiana was not sorry.*

"Okay, I'm not sorry for getting me some, but I am sorry for keeping you up. Please forgive me! And please, get some so you can get some a good nut!"

It was time to announce the winner. *"Oh, I got a woman, remember? I got the woman."*

"Are you telling me you got her into bed?" Georgiana asked. *"I know you danced with her, but you didn't win the bet unless you got her into bed."*

Tina couldn't have entered the room at a more perfect time. *"Good morning,"* she said, leaning in and kissing Diamond on the cheek.

"Good morning, baby," she answered, smirking at Georgiana. Her face was literally green with envy and illness. Diamond thought about calling an ambulance because the bitch looked sick.

"It ain't over," she mouthed at Diamond as she made a hasty exit from the kitchen, not bothering to speak to Tina.

Diamond didn't know what she meant about it not being over. She'd clearly won the bet, and it should have been over. Hell, if she were her, it would have been over when Tina dissed her not once, but twice.

"I don't want to cause any problems for your room-mate and you, so I'm going to leave. Besides, you did say you have to work to do this morning, right?"

"Sadly, I do," Diamond grumbled.

"Are we still on for this evening?" Diamond had promised to cook her a homemade meal before she went to work the club at ten.

"Be here at six o'clock sharp." After a long, passionate kiss, she left; and Diamond went to her room to get dressed for work.

Once Diamond got to work, she didn't even have a minute to breathe. No sooner than she sat down at the console did the crazy calls start. She couldn't believe *people actually called 911 for simple things. A young mother wanted the cops to come over and talk to her seven-year-old because he was out of control. Diamond wanted to tell the woman to get a belt and wear his li'l bad ass out! And then, there was the people who called 911 only to ask the time. She was two seconds from cussing the man out, but since the lines were recorded, that wasn't an option! The officers, of course, weren't much better than the callers. They were all a bunch of banana brains! She had to continuously repeat information that they were too stupid to simply write down. And even after she gave them the addresses three times or more, they still went to the wrong houses! Then, they got an attitude as if it were her fault. "Relax, relate, release" came out of her mouth so many times.*

Diamond was so excited about cooking for Tina that evening. As soon as her relief came in, she briefed them and practically ran to her car. She peeled out of the parking lot and headed over to the supermarket to buy shrimp, tilapia, rice, and fresh string beans. Diamond was sure that Tina would love her seafood feast. At home, she changed into a pair of sweats and started dinner.

"That smells good. What you cooking?" Georgiana asked, having the nerve to peek into her pots and pans.

"I'm making a seafood dinner for Tina."

"Hmm," she mumbled. "So, she's coming over again, huh?"

"Yeah, Georgiana, she is. Believe it or not, some people love thicker, fluffier women." Diamond shrugged her shoulders and for good measure she added, "I guess Tina is one of those people."

"We'll see," she called over her shoulder, switching her hips out of the kitchen. No telling what she meant by that. Knowing Georgiana, it could have been anything.

Tina arrived precisely at six and Diamond was impressed. She was dressed casually in jeans, a nice shirt, and boots. I love me a chick who wears Timbs.

"Baby, that was delicious," she complimented her, after her second helping of the seafood feast.

"I'm glad you liked it. I made it especially for you."

"Careful. A woman could get used to that."

Diamond blushed like a little girl with a bad case of puppy love.

Tina looked into her eyes. "I love your smile, your laugh. It's infectious."

"Well, I have never had anyone make me smile so much." She felt comfortable talking to Tina. Diamond really hadn't felt that way before. "Atinia, I have never felt this comfortable with anyone. Ever."

"I always want you comfortable and content when you are around me. Any other way wouldn't be right," Tina insisted, with a look of honesty in her eyes.

Diamond cleared their dishes from the table. When she returned to the dining room, Tina was standing by the chair waiting for her.

"May I kiss you?" Tina asked, like the shy schoolgirl she had been back in high school.

"I thought you'd never ask."

Diamond drew her lips toward Tina's. The passionate kiss seemed to last for an eternity.

"Now come here." Diamond grabbed her hand and led the way to her bedroom. Once inside the room, Tina dropped to her knees and pulled Diamond's pants and panties off in one motion. She was so glad that she was wearing that long-lasting scent Love Spell by Victoria's Secret. She tenderly kissed her thighs. She felt her desire for her as each kiss placed Tina's lips closer to Diamond's pleasure zone. She could feel herself creaming from pure excitement. She reached down and

placed her hand on the back of Tina's head and gently guided her to her pussy lips. The moment she penetrated Diamond with her tongue, she screamed in pure delight. Her moans of pleasure took the excitement to a new level, and she loved it!

Tina confessed that she loved the very taste of Diamond, the way she felt, the scent of her excited womanhood.

She felt like she was going to explode just from Tina tasting her love juices. She loved her tongue, but she needed Tina to be on top of her.

Tina laid her down gently on the plush bedding and positioned herself over Diamond. She looked into her eyes and leaned down. Whispering in her ear, Tina said, "Diamond, I want you with all that I am and aspire to be. I have wanted you from the very first time I laid eyes on you. Please let me have you."

"Just make love to me, Tina! Make love to me, please!" She wanted to believe Tina, but she was terrified of getting hurt at the same time. Her body wanted her, but her heart was so afraid to let Tina all the way in. Her fear of being hurt must have been obvious, because her body suddenly turned cold.

"Baby, what's wrong?" Tina asked her, when she recognized the fear in her eyes just before entering her.

"Why did you choose me instead of Georgiana?" Diamond asked. Suddenly, she felt self-conscious. She knew that she was a few sizes bigger than Georgiana, and a few shades darker. She didn't always have Georgiana's level of confidence.

"Why wouldn't I?" was Tina's reply. "If I wanted a woman I could spend one night with, I would have chosen Georgiana. Maybe. But, I'm not looking for drama, Diamond. I'm looking for a woman I can hold in my arms and share my life with. I'm ready for love. Are you?"

Before Diamond could answer, her bedroom door opened, and in strode Georgiana, wearing nothing but stilettos. Her raggedy behind bounced all over the place. "This charade has gone far enough, Tina."

"What the fuck?" they asked in unison.

"No one has ever turned down this good pussy before," she boasted as she strutted her nakedness over to them, opening her stank legs in Tina's face. "One taste and you'll be hooked," she cooed, while digging her fingers in between her thighs and trying to press the tip of her wet fingers against Tina's lips.

"Okay, bitch, you've gone too far," Diamond said, springing to her feet. She had a lot of nerve busting up in her room naked, trying to fuck her woman like she wasn't even there! "Tina chose me, not you. Why do you insist on making a fool of yourself?"

Tina stood up from the bed and walked toward the bathroom.

"Look at you, Di! You think she really wants that instead of this?" Georgiana asked, as if she was a supermodel or something.

"You know what, Georgiana, you are out of here!" Diamond yelled. "Get your shit and get up out my house before I throw you out!"

"It's not even that serious. It's not like we haven't done this before," she said loud enough for Tina to hear. "This time you won, but I'm sure she can handle us both."

Tina emerged from the bathroom. "I don't know what kind of games you two are playing, but I'm out."

"Tina, no, wait!" Diamond begged, while Georgiana smiled victoriously.

"Diamond, I didn't know this was a game to you. I thought we were looking for the same thing, but obviously not."

"Tina, let me assure you, you're worth more than a bet to me. It was childish for Georgiana and me to compete for you. You're more than just a one-night stand for me."

"Girl, stop lying. We've done this hundreds of times, and even though I won most of the time, you have had your share of one-night stands."

Georgiana was doing her best to make Tina see Diamond in a negative light. Didn't she tell her to get out already? Why was she still there and sitting her funky ass on Diamond's bed, of all places? Diamond marched over to Georgiana, drew back, and punched her hard across the face.

"Get out!" Diamond yelled as Georgiana ran out yelping like the limp-dick dog she was.

"I hope you can forgive me, Tina." When she didn't answer, Diamond opened her nightstand drawer and pulled out a notebook. "Do you mind if I share a poem with you?" she asked. Tina shrugged her shoulders, and she proceeded to recite a poem about a special world for the two of them.

"That's just how special you are to me," she concluded.

Tina walked closer to her and reached for her hand. "Are you sure you're ready for this? Are you ready for love?"

"Tina, I'm ready. I'm ready for your love."

She laid her down on the bed and slowly finished undressing her. Then she watched as she undressed herself, turning away momentarily to put her clothes on the recliner. When she turned around, her legs were spread eagle. She was rubbing her pussy with one hand, while beckoning her over with the other. She was ready to love again. She was ready to be held and trust that her heart wouldn't be broken again. She not only opened her legs to a lover but opened her heart to a friend.

Tina entered her love tunnel with a thick and doubly pleasurable strap-on, and Diamond was in pure heaven. She kept telling her how she was so wet and tight. Tina was gentle with her until she felt herself drowning in her ecstasy. She thrust deeper into her with more intensity as her pace quickened. She lost all control when she felt her walls squeezing ever so tightly.

They held each other closely as their bodies trembled. An orgasm took over, leaving them both too weak to move from their embrace. But they couldn't stop touching each other. If this is what love feels like, I want to feel this way forever, *Diamond thought. She loved feeling her and she apparently loved feeling her.*

After lying in Tina's arms for a few minutes she had just enough strength to roll over and climb on top of her baby and mount her huge, double-headed dick. Even after all of what they'd done, she rode her for what felt like hours, and loved every second of it! Just as they both were about to release for the final time that night, India.Arie's beautiful voice crooned from the other room as she sang "Ready For Love." Their forever and a day had just begun.

Sadly their forever ended when Tina was murdered just before Diamond's college graduation. It was then and there that she'd decided she'd do anything to avenge her love's death.

Chapter 20

While the trial was taking place, on the other side of the city Prime and C Class were sitting in the chrome Hummer discussing topics of all sorts. Prime still hadn't let C Class or anyone else know about Monica. He couldn't allow anything to jeopardize what he had going. The Double Gs were too well informed and connected. The most minor slip-up could cause a wake of destruction. It wasn't worth the risk. When he was finally in possession of the "G" Files, he would then pull his crew in to carry out the second phase of his plan, which was to sell them to the highest bidder and disappear forever.

C Class was in the driver's seat reading the local newspaper. "These Double G bitches are vicious," he stated. "It's crazy how we put in all of this work, and they're still ahead of us. By light years. And they ain't even no street chicks," he concluded.

"That's what makes 'em dangerous," Prime began to explain. "Most people in this street life don't use their brains. They don't plan; they just react. That's why the FBI is so good at what they do. You need a GED to be a cop, but a college degree to be one of them and they study psychology. This shit is so much deeper than guns and drugs. Those two elements are at the bottom of the food chain. We're the lowest of the food chain. Why? 'Cause we ain't worth shit but prison space to make it all look like America's tough on crime. It's all politics," Prime stated.

"I hear that," C Class agreed as he turned the page. "Damn, I can't believe they rocked li'l shorty like that. That cop's daughter. The feds are relentless," he said, buying into their cover story.

"Don't believe the hype," Prime retorted. "I'm willing to bet you every one of my cars that the Double G bitches pulled that off."

C Class just laughed. "Nah, you givin' 'em too much credit."

"Am I?" Prime rhetorically asked. "Think about it. When did the feds start being stupid? Read the front page for yourself. Why would they pull up to that house in broad daylight, and carry out that hit? If it's one thing I know about the government, it's that they're patient. They'll watch and let a known drug dealer make millions of dollars and then bust 'em. Some investigations last as long as ten years. Nah, that was them heartless bitches," Prime assessed.

"If so, then that means the feds know about it. So it's a war." A sinister grin appeared across C Class's face. "Who you got ya money on?" C Class asked, pulling out a knot of money.

Prime seemed to be in deep thought. *If only you knew, my friend,* Prime said to himself. He managed to match C Class's smile to hide the raw truth. "Right now, I gotta go with them heartless bitches."

"Good. After what you just told me, I'll take the feds for a stack. But what's up with you and them broads, though?"

A confused look appeared on Prime's face. "What the fuck that supposed to mean?"

"Whoa!" C Class threw up his hands. "I don't mean nothin', bruh. I was just asking, 'cause it ain't like you to be giving them bitches that much credit. That's all," C Class offered.

Prime felt stupid for overreacting the way he just had. Ever since the Double Gs tried to catch him slipping he hadn't underestimated any of their capabilities. He knew his reason for jumping the gun on his man. He had been on edge since he had evaded their trap.

"My bad, my dude. I just don't like them dyke bitches!" he apologized. "Them chicks are the worst kind: intelligent, got paper, power, and don't fuck with niggas," he ended.

"It's cool, bruh. And I feel you about them chicks. They may have a strong team, but the muthafuckin' feds always got a stronger one, so my money still on 'em," C Class retorted.

Prime laughed. "Bet!" he confirmed as they shook hands to make it official. Although Prime was betting on the Double Gs, in his mind he was betting against them and, if all went according to plan, he knew the payout would be beyond his wildest dreams.

His thoughts were suddenly distracted by a car pulling up. The powder blue Bentley pulled up along the driver's side of the Hummer. The words from "Vacation," off of Young Jeezy's album *The Recession,* blared out of the speakers. The music lowered along with the front passenger side window. Clips was by himself. "What's good?" he yelled, ducking his head low to see up into the high-sitting Hummer.

Prime sat upright so he could see across C Class.

"Ain't nothing," C Class replied.

"Where the fuck you been? You ain't hardly even around no more. I'ma have to give ya spot to Li'l Smoke and 'em," Prime seriously joked.

"Yeah, right!" Clips brushed off Prime's statement. "I'm working on something major right now. I'm still in da hood like four wings and fried rice, though," he joked. "It's still our city, and I still got shit out here locked. We ain't have no security problems yet, right?"

"Nah," C Class joined in. "But stay on point though," he added.

"That's what I do!" Clips declared as the window rolled up. His music could be heard blasting as he vanished up the block.

Both Prime and C Class shook their heads. "What the fuck's been up with that li'l nigga lately?" Prime asked C Class.

"You noticed too? I thought it was just me. He's been tripping for the last few weeks."

"Word. And he ain't shootin' straight with us. He's talking in circles. What the fuck the riddles about?"

"Who knows," C Class said.

"That's the problem," Prime offered. "We don't," he pointed out. "It's time we figure this shit out. I trust him, but I just don't like when people switch up their routine. There was a time when you couldn't pull this li'l nigga away from the streets. Now he ain't hardly ever around."

"True. What do you suggest?"

"I'ma put Smoke on him. Let Smoke tail him around until we figure out what's going on. It's probably nothing, but you just never know—"

"Until it's too late," C Class finished Prime's sentence.

Chapter 21

"Blade! Legal mail!" The officer rapped his metal key against the glass of Edna Blade's cell door.

For some, doing a life sentence in prison was worse than spending an eternity in a grave. If you asked most women, they'd choose death over a life bid, but that was not thirty-five-year-old Edna Blade's, aka Edge's, decision. She happily accepted life in the Florence McClure Women's Correctional Center in North Las Vegas over the death penalty she would have received for the crimes she had been found guilty and convicted of. She knew with life she still had a fighting chance to see daylight again. Granted, she had done a lot in the streets, none of which she had ever gotten caught for, which was why she had maintained her innocence for the past nine and half years she had been in prison on the charges she was found guilty of. She had enough time on her hands to figure out how she got herself in her predicament and, furthermore, figure out a way to get herself out of it. That's if she could stay alive long enough.

She was locked away amid the most notorious female criminals who had ever stepped foot on Nevada's soil, which meant you had to be cut from a certain type of cloth in order to survive in the women's facility. Edge was not exempt. Although she was well known for her unadulterated ruthlessness, shortly after entering the prison system she had to make many examples out of people, which opened doors for enemies. Once she was done proving her point, people left her alone for the most part, but she was tested every now and again.

She had been in prison almost a full decade; Edge had nearly given up all hope. The only thing that kept her fighting was the hate and revenge she had toward those responsible for putting her where she was. She had been shot down left and right but still she never gave up. All of her appellate remedies had been denied. It had been solidified that she would remain incarcerated until her death.

Edge wondered why she would be getting a manila envelope marked LEGAL MAIL twice in one week from the appellate division. She was already preparing to appeal their decision to a higher court, so as far as she was concerned, there was nothing else to talk about when it came to them. After signing for the mail, Edge tore it open with her good hand and removed the documents. She scanned the heading then studied the content of the letter. Her eyes read with rapid speed. A confused look appeared on her face. *Is this some fucking joke or something?* she questioned. She flipped through the pages and then returned to the first page. Edge's heart began to pound up against her chest. Her eyes began to water as she reread the top lines over and over.

The package Edge had received informed her that her case was being reviewed due to the involvement of the arresting officers, Blake and Douglass. The letter went on to state that most of the cases involving them were immediately being overturned. It went even further to state that Officer Douglass gave a sworn statement where he admitted to planting evidence in Edge's home in order to arrest and convict her. The letter suggested that Edge hire an attorney in an urgent matter to handle the necessary proceedings, which would result in her future release.

Edge almost passed out in her cell. The news was breathtaking. She needed a lawyer quick. She only had one person she could think of to call on for such a favor. Edge prayed that the letter she wrote wasn't still being held against her.

Chapter 22

Club Treasures was not like its normal "turn down for what" atmosphere. It was more like a funeral parlor service. Aside from the DJ and bouncers, the club consisted of three silicone-filled young Caucasian dancers on stage, two barmaids fraternizing among themselves, two more dancers sitting on the laps of two Latino gentlemen, while two others walked the floor in the sprinkle of customers. Had it not been for the presence of and generous order from the Double Gs, it would have been a moneyless day for the establishment.

In the VIP area, over in the corner, were just over thirty members of the Double Gs organization. Six metal buckets of ice consisting of two bottles of flavored Cîroc were aligned at the main table, while the miniature tables each possessed a bottle of the assorted vodka. Diamond had given specific instructions to the club for them not to be disturbed. Since Club Panties had been closed and Starr was not home, as temporary leader of the Double Gs, Diamond felt Treasures was the most comfortable and neutral place to hold a meeting. She knew the Double Gs were all on edge since the arrest of Starr. She figured it would do everyone some good if they all met in a setting where they could have drinks, enjoy music, and chill, like they were used to at their club, while she brought everyone up to speed and handed down orders to a select few.

"I just want to start by saying I love all of my sistas." Diamond held up her flute of amaretto Cîroc.

The rest of the Double Gs joined her by holding up their glasses as well.

"Double Gs for life!" Bubbles chimed.

"Double Gs for life!" the rest of the Double Gs cheered.

Diamond loved to see her sisters in high spirits. She could tell they were charged up. She waited for them to settle before she spoke.

"Right now, some of our sistas are incarcerated," she began. "They are trying to divide us in attempts to weaken us. Planting seeds and watching them grow." Diamond scanned the faces of the Double Gs to see how they took to her words. She looked from Monica to Felicia and then to Bubbles before she continued. "This is a time we show strength and ride for what we believe and who we believe in. The only way they can infiltrate us is if we help them."

Again, Diamond scanned the faces in the room. She was deliberately making statements to get a reaction from someone, something she had learned from being around Starr. "We took an oath that if another violates or crosses us or our family, the consequences and penalties shall be severe and we'd stand by this until we've breathed our last breaths," Diamond recited some of the Double Gs pledge.

As one final time Diamond scanned the sea of faces surrounding her, she noticed all of the Double Gs shared the same expressions of admiration. Although Diamond was pleased by their response to her speech, she knew not every smile was genuine and not every handshake was a friendly one.

"Double Gs for life!" Diamond toasted.

"Double Gs for life!" the members followed.

As the night wound down, Double Gs spilled out of the club. Despite it being dead the entire night, they all had enjoyed themselves. Diamond made her way over to the bar to settle their tab. She eyed the sexy Asian bartender as she rung her up. She was tempted to press her, but decided not to, knowing she had court in the morning. Aside from that she knew she needed to stay focused on the full plate she had in front of her. With Starr being away, Diamond had to quickly step up and fill her lover's shoes as best she could. Diamond signed off on the charge, then placed a hundred dollar bill on top of the check, adding to the barmaid's healthy gratuity. The Asian barmaid lit up. Diamond knew she could have her.

"Another time," Diamond said before exiting the bar.

As she made her way toward the club's exit, something caught her attention from her left peripheral. Diamond noticed the short, obese club owner staring at her. He flashed her a welcoming smile and waved. Diamond returned a short wave and nod of the head. *What the fuck was that all about?* she questioned as she exited the establishment.

Sammy had paced his office back and forth all night. He contemplated whether the time was right. He was hoping the leader, Starr, would have been out by now, but she wasn't. Once he figured out who was in charge now, he wondered if he should take the chance. Every time he pumped himself up to go down and do it he chickened out. As the night came to an end, Sammy knew he was running out of time. Just when he finally worked back up the nerve, he saw her and in a split second his mind had changed once again. All he could do was smile and wave as she strolled by.

"Fuck!" he cursed as soon as Diamond made her way out of his club.

Chapter 23

Starr spent the entire ride back to the federal detention center pissed. She wondered why Diamond hadn't taken a few moments to brief her representation. She knew Diamond had the Spalding trial going on, but she figured Diamond would have at least set aside some time to show up herself just to save face instead of just sticking her with some half-assed lawyer with no balls in a cheap suit. Starr was sure Diamond would get to the bottom of everything and get her out but there was no doubt in her mind that games were being played. Starr knew she couldn't afford to lose her cool and show her hand. Seeing Monica was the only thing that kept her from blacking out on the lawyer and in the courtroom. Monica looked resilient. There was no denying she was physically attracted to her.

As Starr arrived back to the holding facility, she was brought in, stripped, and placed back into her pumpkin-colored jumper. She didn't even care. She was ready to go back to her freezing single cell that she was forced to get used to. To her surprise, she was informed that she would be going upstairs to general population instead, as long as she promised to behave while she was up there. Starr laughed on the inside at how they tried to make it seem like a favor to her, instead of revealing the fact that they couldn't legally justify holding her in the "dry cell" for much longer. She knew with Diamond as her lawyer, it would only be a matter of time before they started playing fair before they jeopardized whatever they thought they had on her.

The feds purposely requested that Starr be sent to the roughest women's pod. Starr was escorted down the long tunnel and into an elevator, along with two young white girls who had been arrested for seven counts of check fraud and ten counts of identity theft. Based on the conversation she had heard, Starr discovered that the one girl, Kathy, a short, pale-skinned, redheaded girl with a pretty face and ass and hips like a sista, was charged with a breach of federal security. She was a vicious computer geek turned hacker and could practically break through the digital firewalls of any security system she wanted. She had been all through the FBI's and the CIA's personal databases, just to finish a report for her midterm paper.

Margaret, a shapely and busty pale-skinned blonde, with hips like a black girl and the height and posture of a model, was the one who put the plan together. Kathy and Margaret were juniors attending the same college. When Margaret learned of Kathy's skills, she began to manipulate her into pulling off white-collar scams. Margaret was the brains. It was apparent to Starr that neither of them were the muscle of their operation. She could tell they were both terribly frightened. Starr watched both girls clutch their bedrolls tight during the entire elevator ride to the eighth floor.

The female guard led all three of them out into the hall. Starr chuckled to herself as she heard Kathy whisper to Margaret in the shakiest voice, "I hear women rape other women in here."

Margaret visibly lost her breath. She looked back at Kathy with fearful confirmation. "And that's only if you're lucky. There's no telling what else they might do," she replied.

"Keep it moving!" the guard yelled, pushing them down the hall.

The three women approached a glass bubble with a closed sliding door. An elderly male guard sat behind a tinted glass. He was usually asleep, or at least nodding off, half drunk. The camera monitors he was supposed to be viewing to make sure that both sides of the pods he sat between ran smoothly were usually unattended. The female inmates pretty much did what they wanted to do with no regard, knowing he wasn't doing his job. But today he was wide awake.

He pressed a button and the outer doors of the bubble slid open. All three girls entered with a guard. The door slid closed behind them. There were two more sliding doors, one on the right and one on the left. A voice came over the loud speaker, asking the girls to approach the tinted glass and call out their names and ID numbers on the inmate ID cards they were given.

Margaret went first as the female guard stood behind them. "Margaret Shalloway. 02562-702," she announced, reading the number off the card.

The voice shot back through the speaker, "Pod B, to your right. Cell eighteen, upper bunk. Next."

Kathy nervously approached the tinted glass. "Katherine States. 02536-702," she stated without reading the card. At a glance she had it all memorized and locked in her memory. She was a wizard when it came to numbers. She turned to her right and began to walk over to join Margaret.

The voice shot through the speaker again: "Pod A. To your left. Cell fifty-seven, tier two, upper bunk. Next."

Kathy immediately panicked. "Noooo! I'm with her. Noo. Please no," she cried. "There has to be some mistake."

"No mistake! Next!" the voice over the speaker clarified. The female guard stopped up front and pulled Kathy away from Margaret, who was tearing up.

Starr approached the window. "Starrshma Fields, 63660-702."

"Pod A, tier two, cell fifty-seven, lower bunk."

Pod B's door slid open and Margaret was escorted through. She turned and watched Kathy and Starr enter the other side.

Once inside, the girls were on their own. The female guard who ushered them in left without any instructions. Starr figured it out for herself.

"Fresh meat," a female heckler called out.

Starr laughed to herself. *Please don't let me have to hurt one of these bitches in here,* she reasoned in her mind. She could see the catcall had Kathy shaken up. "Ignore them. They're just trying to scare you," Starr offered. "Come on, I guess we're roommates. Follow me," Starr declared.

Kathy pulled up on her and followed directly behind her every step. She was so pigeon-toed she somewhat waddled when she walked.

Cell fifty-seven was located all the way in the back corner on the left side of the top tier. The tier wrapped around the pod in the shape of a big U. Televisions hung from the ceiling. Many women inmates were on the first level watching the different screens. There were many tables in the middle of the floor where many of them played spades and poker, and drew pictures. There was also a Ping-Pong table far in the back, and a recreation deck that was like a caged outside balcony. The girls were allowed to go out for fresh air and get a fenced view of the city. The Spanish girls played handball against the brick wall, and the black girls played basketball. The white girls just tried to be seen and not heard.

Starr and Kathy headed to their room. The walk was long and cluttered. Many of the oversized women purposely stood in the way of the new arrivals as a scare tactic. None of their faces were welcoming. It didn't bother Starr one bit. But Kathy was practically walking with her eyes closed.

When Starr finally pulled up on their cell, the door was already cracked. Without thought, she just pushed it open. She almost couldn't contain her laughter. She cleared her throat and asked, "Am I interrupting something? We could come back a little later if y'all would like," she added.

She scanned the spacious cell. Two women on the bottom bunk were engaged in a sexual activity, while two other women were at the cell's desk sniffing lines of a white powdered substance off of a playing card. They were so startled that they spilled it onto the floor by accident. One of them quickly dropped to the ground and began snorting it off the floor.

"Bitch! Look what you made me do. You owe me fifty dollars," she proclaimed.

A sinister grin appeared on Starr's face. She stepped in closer to the young, light-skinned slim girl named Darlene. She could tell that she was once pretty before she fell victim to drugs. Starr's first instinct was to bash the young girl's face in, but she sided against it, knowing she didn't need to make matters any worse than they already were. Still, she refused to pass up the chance to put the girl in her place.

"You can take it out of the hundred dollars you owe me for the hotel fees," Starr snarled. All four of the unwanted guests were equally shocked by Starr's words. The two on the bed were so intimidated by Starr's boldness that they climbed out of the bed, gathered their clothes, and began to dress. By now, Erica, the other drug user, was on her feet.

Kathy stood behind Starr as if she was her shadow. She was praying that the incident resolved itself peacefully, but she was unsure as to what she would do if it didn't.

Darlene studied Starr, who towered over her. She had been in many battles in her young twenty-three-year-old life to know how to pick and choose them. Something in her gut told her this was one of those days when she should choose wisely.

Starr could tell the girl was weighing her options. She also could tell Erica was Darlene's henchman, which meant she would be the first one Starr would target if Darlene made the wrong choice. The tension was so thick in the air you could slice it with a knife. A dead silence also filled the air. Starr's and Darlene's eyes locked. Starr could already see the light-skinned girl's answers in her eyes before she opened her mouth. She knew the eyes never lied.

"Come on, yo. It's almost count time anyway." Darlene reached for Erica's hand.

"We'll see you later, bitch!" Erica barked.

Starr stood there in silence. She didn't bother to move out of the their way, either. She felt some type of way about the messy cell. Starr was tempted to make them return to the cell and clean it up. It looked like it had been used as a drug house and whorehouse all weekend.

Kathy was hiding behind Starr the entire time. When she finally heard silence, she poked her head out. Starr looked back at her to say something, but instead her line of vision was drawn over the tier, down to the first floor. She caught a glimpse of the young black male correctional officer exiting cell twenty-nine. What drew her attention was the fact that he was tucking his shirt in and the lights were out in the cell. Seconds later, Starr peeped a female poke her head out of the door, watching him leave; and then she shut it. Her focus was distracted by the blaring sound of another officer's voice.

"Count time! Count time!" the CO yelled. All of the females scrambled back to their cells and locked in. Starr made a mental note of what she had seen.

Chapter 24

"I'm sorry, Tom. I just can't get a hold of that kind of money. My superior will never sign off on it," Mobley explained to Agent McCarthy as they sat in his top floor office.

Agent McCarthy was stressed. He didn't know what to do, or where else to turn. "Please," he begged. His eyes began to tear up. Ronald Mobley had never seen him so distraught. "You gotta help me. Look at all of the money we seized in the last six months alone. I've personally put half of it right back on the streets myself. Ron, they only gave her three weeks. That's all she has left if nothing else is done. You've met her; she doesn't deserve this. Not her, Ron. Anyone but her. They say that if she doesn't get the right treatment soon, the process will be irreversible, and there's nothing anyone could do. Nothing at all. We need help now, Ron. Now," he declared as he stood up from the seat.

Chief Officer Mobley shook his head in empathy. He stared out his office window into deep space. He was unable to look Agent McCarthy in his eyes, wishing it weren't either one of them in the position they were in.

"I can't make any promises, Tom. And the chances are slim, but I'll make a few more calls, track down a few favors, and add some real pressure on anyone I think can help."

"Thanks. That's all I ask." The two shook hands. Agent McCarthy got up and exited his superior officer's office.

He took one glance back at the office door. He was torn between his morals and oath as a man and officer of the law and his emotions and oath as a father. *I hope you can make something happen for my family. For all of our sakes,* he ended his thoughts with.

Chapter 25

Officer Douglass sat in the protective custody cell in tears. He just couldn't forgive himself for what had happened to the only two people he loved. A guard came in and informed him that he would be able to attend the funeral of his wife and daughter, but he would be shackled and restrained. Officer Douglass realized that he had to take the good with the bad. But there was no good. The steel around his wrists, waist, and ankles would be a reminder to all at the funeral that it was his own actions that caused such horrific tragedy. It was his hands their blood was on. But there was no way he wasn't going to attend his final chance to say good-bye.

Chapter 26

Starr traded bunks with Kathy. She preferred to be on the top. She knew statistically in jail the person who slept on the bottom was much easier to get attacked first if something ever kicked off. She didn't let Kathy know that. After they both cleaned up and disinfected the cell, without uttering a word to each other, Kathy made her bed and curled up in the corner of it. She buried her face between her knees, sobbing. Her sobs echoed in Starr's ears.

Starr looked down at Kathy. "What's wrong? Cryin' ain't gonna set you free. Maybe if you were in front of the judge. But in here, you gotta be strong, or they'll swallow you whole out there."

Kathy began wiping her face. "You're right, but . . ." Kathy sniffled as she began to spill her guts and fill Starr in on every last detail. Starr listened attentively. She was impressed at the skill set of her cellmate but didn't let her know.

"You can do all of that with a computer?" was all Starr asked once Kathy was done telling her all her business. Starr saw a bigger picture in front of her.

"All I need is an iPhone or a BlackBerry," Kathy revealed, smiling for the first time. "What about you?" she inquired.

Starr thought long and hard before answering. "Taxes," she lied. Kathy was too green not to believe her. She decided to take Kathy under her wing for as long as she could. She knew in due time she would reveal what she really wanted to Kathy, but until then she would keep her on a need-to-know basis.

The count was cleared and the shift had changed. A female guard was working the second shift, which was 4:00 p.m. to midnight. Their cell door unlocked.

"Chow time!" the guard yelled, signaling dinner call.

"Let's go eat," Starr said, not really wanting to. But she wanted Kathy to come out of the cell. She knew that if she left it up to her, Kathy would stay in that bed and starve to death. She needed her to stay healthy and get stronger.

The dinner line was long. Kathy and Starr made light, casual conversation as they waited at the back of it. From afar, Starr noticed two familiar faces speaking to each other, but she showed no reaction. They didn't seem to notice her. She went back to conversing with Kathy. In a short amount of time, she had taken a liking to her. Kathy was an innocent child in so many ways, Starr thought. She just needed better guidance. Starr was convinced that she wanted to recruit Kathy.

They finally got to the head of the line and got their trays consisting of meatloaf, mashed potatoes, and green beans. After what Starr had been seeing all weekend, it didn't look so bad. Kathy, who was looking for a place to sit, trailed behind Starr. All of the tables seemed to be filled. Starr spotted one table in particular wide open.

"Come on," Starr instructed.

Kathy followed as they climbed down the small flight of steps and walked past the many tables filled with women. The poker table was dead in the center. The entire pod instantly grew silent, as they watched the two new girls sit down. Kathy could feel the sudden change. She became too nervous to eat. She felt every single eyeball individually piercing through her pale, 190-pound body. Starr, on the other hand, ignored it all. She was hungry and didn't waste any time eating.

"Eat your food. Don't worry about them," she ordered Kathy.

Kathy stared at her food like a little girl. She was barely twenty-one years old, and had made it to college early by skipping a grade and a half. She toyed around with the meatloaf, picking at it with a small plastic fork, and then she proceeded to take small bites. Starr smiled with approval.

However, it didn't take long for their private feast to be interrupted. A large shadow appeared over Kathy's body. She paused from eating. She was too intimidated to turn around. She felt a strong, manly hand grip her shoulder. Starr looked up and saw a large, dark, heavy-set black woman with two French braids hanging over a blue bandana. Starr paid her no mind. She brushed her uninvited presence off and lowered her head back into her plate as the large woman stared both her and Kathy down. Within seconds, groups of girls with matching bandanas gathered behind the large woman as she spoke in a masculine voice.

"See, y'all new. So y'all get a pass. But y'all got five minutes to get up and find somewhere else to sit," she declared.

Starr looked over at Kathy who had now turned bright red. She was too scared to finish swallowing the food halfway down her throat because of the lump in the way. Starr chuckled lightly. She then looked up at the brawly woman.

"Orrr what?" Starr nonchalantly asked.

The large woman was shocked by such an audacious reply. She began to laugh. As a scare tactic, she began cracking her knuckles and palmed her balled-up fist. "Orrr y'all gonna get sent to the infirmary without your teeth." She spoke in a more aggressive tone, finishing the answer to Starr's question.

"Oh!" Starr sarcastically smirked and nodded. "Well, why didn't you just say so then?" She then lowered her head back into her plate and began eating, ignoring the woman, showing blatant disrespect.

Light laughter could be heard all around Big Wanda. She had been publicly played. She knew she had to react quickly. She didn't think a victory over the Amazon-figured woman would be easier than it would be against the fat white girl, so she went for the weaker of the two. She gripped Kathy's left collarbone and lifted her up over the seat. Kathy was so terrified that she turned and threw up all over Big Wanda.

"Bitch!" Big Wanda yelled.

Starr burst into laughter. She was enjoying herself. Kathy swiftly maneuvered around the table and hid behind Starr, eyeing the wild pack of women in dire need of makeovers. Starr remained calm, still smiling. She folded her arms and crossed her legs as she counted backward from ten under her breath. "Three, two, one," she uttered.

Just as Big Wanda was about to make her move, she felt a thin breeze of wind brush across her left cheek. None of her crew seemed to notice the two women creep up and break through the group headed in Big Wanda's direction. What happened took a minute to register. By the time it did, it was too late.

"Nooooo!" Big Wanda cried out hysterically. She cupped her face with her left hand. She could feel her palm getting warm. Big Wanda's eyes nearly bulged out of her head as blood poured through her fingers. She looked at the two women gripping straight razors in each of their hands. She also noticed the rest of her crew attempting to run for cover, but they were chased back to the middle of the floor by six more double razor-bearing girls.

"You cut me, bitch!" Big Wanda screamed, purposely trying to draw the attention of the guard, who was far away and deep into her conversation.

Starr stood up and told Kathy to stay put. She then directed her attention to the two familiar faces. "Fall back, Gs. I got this." She walked up to Big Wanda and smacked her hard across the face. The blow caused the fresh wound to open even wider. Every viewer cringed and flinched as the blood splashed across Big Wanda's huge face. Big Wanda tried to swing back, but it was too late. Starr had grabbed a firm hold of both of her French braids and pulled down as hard as she could until Big Wanda's head banged off of the table. The impact knocked her out cold. Big Wanda's wolf pack dispersed as fast as they could.

The razor-bearing girls huddled up and began to chant the infamous oath they had taken years ago, the words that planted fear in every other female inmate's soul.

"Double Gs for life! Double Gs for life!" They sang nonstop as Starr stood over Big Wanda. She repeatedly smacked her to wake her up just in time to hear the sounds of her incarcerated Double Gs sisters' chant.

Big Wanda rolled over. Her face was in a pool of her own blood and Kathy's vomit, mixed. She lay on her back, dizzy, wondering what had just happened. Starr was squatting over her.

"Hey, you." She tapped Big Wanda on the cheek lightly. "Go have one of my girls stitch you up," she told her.

Big Wanda was still somewhat dazed. She wondered who the new female inmate was who had just managed to strip her of her reputation of four years of a gangster on the pod. She slowly attempted to make it to her feet. She stared at Starr oddly. As if to read her mind, Starr reached for her arm to help her up.

"By the way, let me introduce myself." She leaned in to Big Wanda's ear. "My name is Starrshma Fields; you may know me as Starr." There was a split-second pause before Starr finished: "Of the Double Gs."

The reaction Big Wanda's eyes made from the introduction was evident she very familiar with both the name and the organization. Everyone stared from afar, each woman with nearly the same question: who was the new inmate? They had all seen the look on Big Wanda's face when Starr had said something in her ear. They all knew whatever was said, it was enough to put fear in the woman who they had all feared since their stay at the facility. They all watched as Starr gave approving nods to the blade-strapped women, who up until then had kept a low profile, had never had any confrontations, and had been no factors on the pod. They watched as Starr made her way back over to the table that once belonged to Big Wanda, sat back down, and went back to eating her meal.

The look on Kathy's face was of pure admiration. She too wondered who Starr really was, but dared not to ask. Although she was young, Kathy was smart enough to know that timing was everything with a woman like Starr. Now was not the time or place, thought Kathy. Everybody returned to their respective places without further incident.

The second half of the day went like it was supposed to. After the wild episode died down, Starr got the respect she deserved. The other inmates finally began to recognize her. She had looked much different after the wild weekend in an orange jumpsuit. They began to match her face with the one they had constantly seen on the news and in the papers recently. It was safe to say Big Wanda wasn't running things anymore. It was unanimous; Starr was the new head bitch in charge now. Every so-called and wannabe female thug now fought for Starr's attention and approval, hoping they'd be among the chosen to become a Double G. Not that it meant anything to her.

She just sat inside her cell speaking with Kathy as the other five Double Gs bikers stood in front of her cell on guard. Big Wanda was in her cell getting stitched up with dental floss by the sixth biker.

Starr and Kathy were sitting on the lower bunk playing gin as Kathy expressed her feelings during the altercation between Starr and Big Wanda. "I was so scared. I thought she was going to murder me after I threw up all over her." Kathy held her cards against her chest with her left hand as she covered her mouth with her right hand, laughing.

"I thought she was going to too. That's why I drew her attention to me," Starr revealed.

"Sooooo taxes, huh?" Kathy felt it was a better time to inquire, with fewer eyes and ears around.

"Well, I didn't exactly lie. They're checking into my club's financial records."

"So, what's the Double Gs all about?" Kathy felt comfortable enough to ask.

Starr studied her, evaluating her intentions for asking before answering. She gave her as much information as she could, without incriminating herself. She wasn't sure if the room was bugged. She still gave Kathy a lot to swallow, and she seemed to be intrigued.

"Wow. You guys, I mean girls, sound well organized and aren't scared of anything," she idolized.

Starr paused and stared at her stone-faced. "Kathy, always remember this: courage isn't the absence of fear. It's just the willpower to triumph over it."

Kathy appreciated the jewel that Starr had just dropped on her. But she desperately wanted to move on to the next subject. "So you really never had sex with a man?" Starr then broke down her close call of molestation and rape to Kathy, who then understood why it was so easy for her to not desire the touch of a man and preferred a woman's.

"So what about kids? None of you will ever have any?"

"No, it's impossible. I guess we could go to a sperm bank. It wouldn't exactly be breaking the rules. But it wouldn't represent what we do, either. Especially what it is we're trying to accomplish. I would love to have a daughter. But it's impossible."

"But you have a mother and father out there somewhere right?"

For a few seconds, Starr thought of what she knew of her family tree. The thoughts had been long buried and were painful to even think about them. Starr shook off the short trip down memory lane. "What about you? You ever had sex?" she redirected the subject.

Kathy blushed bright red and looked down into her lap. "No. I'm too much of a nerd to have a boyfriend. I do like boys, though. Not one in particular. Mostly the ones I see on TV."

"You might make it to be one of us after all," Starr teased.

"Really?!" Kathy asked with excitement. "Could I, like, shoot people 'n' stuff?"

Starr laughed. "Slow down, Angelina Jolie. This ain't the movies. No, I seriously doubt that's for you." She had other plans for Kathy.

"Would I have to date a girl?" she asked with a frowned face.

"Nope. Just don't date a man," Starr honestly retorted.

"I wouldn't mind staying a virgin forever. So, do y'all like jump me, like a street gang or something? How do I get in?" Kathy became more inquisitive.

Starr waited until Kathy ended her babbling. "In due time, young'un'," Starr stated. "No need to run down and fuck one of them. Better to take your time and walk down and fuck them all," Starr added. She couldn't believe she had just quoted Queen Fem's metaphor. She couldn't help but smile admirably at the thought.

Her thoughts were interrupted by the sound of her name being called. "Fields! Visit!" the female guard yelled up from the lower tier.

Starr dropped the cards on the bed and jumped up. She knew who her visitor was or, rather, who she expected it to be. She ran over to the sink to wet her hair and brush her teeth. She gathered her small bag of personal care items and ran down the tier to take a shower that was long overdue.

When Starr returned to the room, she was surprised to see some of the Double Gs bikers in her cell. The one who had sliced Big Wanda in the face was kicking it with Kathy. One of them had some makeup items spread out on the desktop. The Spanish super-sized J-Lo lookalike looked at Starr smiling. "C'mon, gurrrl. You not lookin' like our boss. Lemme see if I can hook you up real quick," Selena stated.

Starr sat on the desk under the light as Dominique stood between her legs and dolled her up. When she was done, Starr looked like her old self. Another Double Gs biker brought in a form-fitting two-piece orange suit. Starr slid into it.

"Hold Kat down while I'm gone," she ordered the Double Gs members.

"With our life, mama," Dominique replied for the rest of them.

Kathy smiled, not only at Dominique's words but also because of the nickname Starr had just given her.

The visiting floor was packed with all women. Starr was escorted in. She searched for Diamond's beautiful face. She was caught off guard by Monica's flawless smile and soft hand gesture waving her over to the awaiting table. Starr strutted over to the section where Monica had been standing. They both embraced in a warm, friendly hug that quickly transpired into a strong, passionate, long-lasting one. They were briefly the center of attention. Starr noticed and broke free of Monica's embrace.

"How are you?" Monica asked as they sat across from each other.

"Pretty good. You know. Making friends," she sarcastically retorted. They shared a laugh.

"It's good to see you. I miss you," Monica reestablished.

"I miss y'all too. I should be out on my next bail hearing, though. Where's Diamond?"

Monica shrugged her shoulders in a nonchalant manner. "No one has seen her. She started that big trial and been MIA."

Starr jumped right into what had been on her mind since Saturday. "What about the other thing? You cool?"

Monica lowered her head, knowing Starr was referring to the recent murders of Loretta and Cameron Douglass. What Monica didn't know was that Starr was testing her to see if she wanted to elaborate. Monica's instincts kicked in. She knew she had to answer. She lifted her head up and stared Starr in her eyes.

"What had to be done was." She left it at that, before quickly changing the subject. "So what do you want me to take care of next?"

Starr smiled. *Cute. I like that,* Starr thought. Monica's response was one of the reasons why Starr was attracted to her. *Always on your toes, I see,* Starr continued with her thought. She could feel the eagerness to prove herself reeking from Monica. *Your wish is my command,* Starr concluded her thoughts, as she leaned in and shared just the mission she had in mind.

Chapter 27

Linda McCarthy dragged herself into the hospital half exhausted. Today had seemed twice as long as any other. She was glad she had brought Victoria in for extra help. There was no way she could've taken the Spalding case head-on by herself. Not with all of the distractions going on.

As she walked in Charlie's private room, Tom was on his knees, holding Charlie's hand to his mouth, kissing and rubbing it as she remained unresponsive. He had been in that same position for hours. He cut his eyes back to the door as Linda entered, and he stood up to hug her. Linda then set her attention on her suffering daughter, whose life was fighting against the clock. She walked over to her and stroked her face, deeply saddened by Charlie's silence. Charlie's face was still bright purplish blue; every vein in her skin was showing. Linda burst into tears. Tom rushed around to the other side of the bed and wrapped his arms around her to console her. The situation was devastating to them both. Something had to be done. Their daughter was dying right before their very eyes and, as of the moment, nothing could be done to help her.

Chapter 28

Diamond sat impatiently twiddling her thumbs. *Why am I here?* she asked herself for the millionth time.

She knew it was more out of curiosity than anything that made her agree to come and meet with someone she vowed to never speak to again. It had been a long time since Diamond Morgan felt the way she was feeling right now. There were only two people in the world who could make her feel the type of way she was feeling now: one was Starr and the other interrupted her thoughts as soon as she walked up to the Plexiglas partition.

Diamond rolled her eyes at the familiar smile. Once upon a time, that was all it would have taken to melt her heart like fried ice cream on a hot summer day. Diamond's eyes followed until her visitor sat down and picked up the phone hanging on the side of the wall. Diamond studied them. *The years have been good to her,* she thought as she admired Edge's physique and beehive brush cut. It looked as if she hadn't aged a day within the past nine years and some change. She hesitantly accepted her visitor's gesture and picked up the receiver on her end.

"Long time," the smooth voice cooed. "You look good," Edge added.

"Why am I here, Edge?" Diamond asked, calling Edna Blade by the name she once fell in love with.

"You tell me," Edge replied.

"Same ol' Edge." Diamond hung up the phone, stood, and started making tracks out of the Ad Seg visiting room. The rapid banging on the glass caused her to stop in her tracks and she spun around. Edge was on the other side of the glass, begging and pleading with the sad puppy eyes Diamond used to find adorable and irresistible. Diamond's head lowered. She shook it and then raised her head back up. She made her way back over to the visiting cubicle. She picked up the phone and sat down.

"You got five minutes," Diamond stated.

"All I need is one," Edge rebutted. Rather than talk, she pulled out the letter she had received in the mail and placed it on the glass.

"I got a shot at a second chance," Edge blurted out even before Diamond could finish reading.

With each line, Diamond's emotions ran wild. She couldn't believe her eyes. Not just because Edge had an opportunity to get a taste of freedom when she had been counted out, but also because of the involvement of Douglass and his partner, which she did not know about. *How could I have slipped up like this?* she questioned herself. All these years, Diamond believed Edge to be guilty of the crimes she had vowed not to commit when they were involved with each other. Now here it was that Edge may have very well been telling the truth the entire time and Diamond refused to believe her. It was the reason why Diamond had turned her back on Edge. It was also the reason why Diamond had abandoned her love for her and built a new one for Starr. A sense of guilt swept through Diamond's body. *Fucking pigs!* Diamond cursed Douglass and his crooked partner.

She couldn't help but think about the possibilities for a moment. Life was great for her and Edge prior to Edge's conviction for killing and cutting up the elderly women according to the news and police. She and Edge had discussed not tampering with the witnesses of the case she had pending. Diamond remembered it as if it were yesterday, when the pictures of the two elderly women flashed across her television screen.

After listening to the gruesome murders, Diamond had immediately picked up the phone and dialed Edge. The fact Edge's phone had gone straight to voice mail, when it usually always rang, was the first red flag for Diamond. The next red flag was when Edge came strolling in the next morning with what Diamond believed to be a look of guilt written all over her face after she had been calling and waited up for her all night. What put the nail in the coffin was the fact that Diamond had noticed Edge had on something different than the jeans and tee she had worn the previous morning she had left the house. Diamond immediately went into interrogation mode and could see right through Edge's lies. When the police came to her house, which was Edge's last known address, and took her away, Diamond didn't even bother to investigate the situation. She had already charged and convicted Edge in her mind.

Diamond shook her head as she revisited the last time she had seen Edge and the two of them were face to face. The sound of Edge's voice through the receiver brought Diamond back to reality. Diamond drew her attention back to Edge. Edge sensed that she was in deep thought and hadn't heard a word she had said.

"I said, I know what you're thinking," Edge repeated.

Diamond rolled her eyes. "And what's that?" she asked dryly. She was still battling with her emotions as she took everything in.

Edge became more serious. "You're thinking about the day I lied to you," she announced.

"So, you do admit that you lied," Diamond was surprised she had said that.

"Yes," Edge replied.

"So what the hell am I doing here?" Diamond hopped up for a second time. Just as Diamond was about to slam the receiver back on its hook, Edge hopped up out of her seat as well.

"Because I didn't lie about that!" Edge chimed. Her words penetrated the Plexiglas and were loud enough for Diamond to hear. Diamond's eyes widened.

"Now please, sit and let me explain," Edge asked, lowering her tone.

Diamond stared at her for a moment. Edge made a gesture with her hand for her to have a seat. Diamond sucked her teeth but did as she was instructed.

"I'm listening," she said nonchalantly.

"I don't know why I lied that morning. I knew I could be truthful with you and we could get past it, but I didn't want to hurt you."

"Are you fucking serious?" Diamond jumped in. "It was all over the news, Edge. You didn't think I'd find out?"

Edge shook her head in frustration. "You're not listening to me!" Her voice grew louder again. "I didn't kill those fucking women, Di!" she added, referring to Diamond by the nickname she had given her.

If there was ever a time when she was confused, it was now. A frown appeared across Diamond's face. "So, what did you lie about then, Edge?"

Edge took a deep breath. It was a question she had wanted to answer for years but had never gotten the chance. She believed that if she would have just come clean back then, things would have played out differently and she and Diamond would still be living happily ever after; but she didn't want to risk losing her, which ended up being the case. Edge knew at that point she had nothing else to lose by revealing the truth.

"I lied about where I was that night," Edge started out with. "Yes, I did go against what you had said about leaving them two old ladies be and I went anyway."

Diamond looked Edge dead in her eyes as she spoke.

"I went over there and I sat and waited. I sat there and drank a whole bottle of Jose Cuervo until they came home. The more I drank, the more I heard your voice in my ear though." Edge took a brief pause as if she was playing the tapes back in her mind. "Between you being the voice of reason and my drunk ass, I abandoned the idea." Edge brushed the top of her head with her hand then ran her palm down her face. She grimaced as her eyes met with Diamond's. "I should've just brought my ass home after that," Edge spat.

Her behavior had Diamond eager to hear the rest of the story. She was now on the edge of her seat. "Where'd you go?" Diamond demanded to know.

"Pst!" was all Edge could muster up as she shook her head.

"That's not an answer, Edge," Diamond replied. Her annoyance was apparent. "Stop beating around the damn bush and tell me what the hell happened!"

"Fuck it!" Edge cursed. "I went to the broad Ebony crib that night," she blurted out.

Diamond stared at Edge oddly. She knew Edge was telling the truth. She didn't know whether she should be mad at herself or at Edge. *You lied to protect some bitch?* Diamond wondered. She didn't want to believe her ears. She closed her eyes and let out a light chuckle. She shook her head for a second time as her chuckle turned into laughter, only it was not a humorous laugh.

"Almost ten years, Edge." It was more of a statement than a question. "Ten years with an eternity to go! And for what?" Diamond's tone grew stronger. "Over some dumb-ass bitch!"

Edge sat there in silence. She knew she deserved whatever Diamond threw her way. She had actually felt a lot better since confessing to her ex-lover. It was if a ten-year-old weight had been lifted off of her shoulders.

Edge watched as Diamond battled with her thoughts. She was tempted to say something but Diamond beat her to the punch and broke the silence.

"Tsk! What's done is done. That was then and this is now." Diamond pulled herself together. *No need to cry over spilled milk,* she concluded. Still, there were unanswered questions she needed clarity on. "So, how did they find your favorite knife at the crime scene, Edge?" she wanted to know.

"Honestly, that's what I've been playing in my head for years," Edge admitted. "The only explanation I could come up with is that I must've dropped it on some drunk shit when I went over there. I didn't realize I didn't have it until I pulled up to the house that morning. I just fig-ured I left it in my jeans at ol' girl's crib. I was still hung over and told myself I'd get it later," Edge stated. "Shit! I really didn't know what the fuck was going on when they came and got me that morning. I thought you were mad at me because I stayed out all night, figured you'd come bail me out or something later and I'd come clean. When I got down to the precinct and they told me what I was being charged with, I flipped the fuck out!"

Edge's demeanor changed as she relived the ordeal. "Then when I called you and you refused my calls, that's when it dawned on me that you thought I was guilty. I never got to explain," Edge recalled. "And that's the truth, the whole truth, and nothing but the truth." Edge touched her tongue with her pointer finger then made an X on her chest. "Cross my heart, hope to die. Stick a needle in my eye."

Diamond tried to hold it in but she couldn't resist. A huge smile flashed across her face. Edge's actions took her back in time to the good old days. She always broke out into giggles like a schoolgirl whenever Edge went through the childhood ritual to prove she was telling the truth.

Edge matched Diamond's smile. "There it is!" Edge pointed out. "That smile that I so love and been keeping me going all these years."

Diamond's smile widened and then quickly disappeared. "Okay, I believe you," Diamond said abruptly. "You don't have to keep pulling out the big guns." She smirked. "I'm going to help you."

Diamond's words caused Edge to light up like a Christmas tree. "Thank you, Di," an excited Edge replied. "Thank you, thank you. Thank you!" she chanted.

"Don't thank me yet," Diamond told her. "First let me get you out of here." Diamond looked from left to right before she finished her statement. "And then you're going to owe me. Big time!" she ended. She was already thinking about the benefit of having Edge back on the streets. Although she was not a Double G, Diamond knew hands down Edge was just as equally thorough, if not more, than any of the Double Gs members, including herself.

"You get me outta here, I do whatever, whenever, however you want me to," Edge stated with conviction in her tone.

Diamond smiled and nodded. "Don't worry. In due time. But first things first," Diamond retorted.

Chapter 29

On the way back from her visit, Starr was feeling like she had never felt before. Even the female guard who escorted her back to her pod had noticed that Starr couldn't stop smiling. There was something so special about Monica. Whatever it was was beginning to override her suspicions, contradicting her better judgment.

As Starr stepped back through the glass bubble and entered the pod, the atmosphere seemed much different than when she had left. The first thing Starr noticed as she looked down the long stretch of the first level was Big Wanda sitting at the poker table with a large white patch over her left cheek. Her group of girls surrounded her as they watched the card game going on. Three of the Double Gs were playing as the other three stood behind them, overseeing the intense poker game, making sure nobody was cheating. Two other Italian girls sat across from them. As far as the other inmates, they were all watching TV, or were outside on the rec deck. For some reason, something just didn't seem right. Then it finally dawned on her.

"Dom!" Starr yelled over toward the card game.

The sound of her voice caused the entire dayroom to turn attention toward Starr.

"Wassup, boss?" a concerned Dominique asked, walking over to Starr.

"Where's Kat?" she asked.

The mention of her name caused Dominique's eyes to grow wide. "*Ay dios mio!*" Dominique exclaimed.

Starr shook her head. She rushed upstairs and speed-walked down the tier. When she got to her room door, she slowed down. The door was already slightly cracked, and the lights were out. She knew there was no way Kathy would be in there alone like that. She burst in with authority. Dominique trailed.

"Get the fuck away from her!" Starr demanded.

Darlene and Erica were startled by Starr and Dominique's sudden presence. It was their intent to be in and out but somehow they had lost track of time. They hadn't realized they had been in the cell so long. They both froze in their tracks. Darlene had Kathy's long hair gripped with one hand, in attempts to force Kathy's nose by the back of her head into the small pile of white powder that sat in the crease of the folded playing card. She had been trying to make a fighting Kathy sniff the cocaine, to no avail, after she had fondled and forced herself on her. Erica stood behind Kathy, awaiting her turn to rape her. *This little young bitch still ain't learned her lesson from earlier,* Starr concluded.

Ironically, Starr hated drug addicts. She felt they didn't respect anything or anyone, and would sell their soul for a dose of their drug of choice.

"This ain't none of your concern," Darlene boldly announced.

"Yeah, mind your business," Erica backed her friend up.

"Yo, who the fuck you junkie bitches think you talkin' to?" Dominique intervened.

Starr silenced Dominique with the wave of her hand. She knew the drugs had both girls feeling courageous. She also knew they were too young to have really heard about who she was and represented. Starr had given Darlene a courtesy pass when they had first met because of that, but she was not sure if she would extend another one to her or her partner. Starr stood there, while Darlene rocked back and forth and turned to her crimey for more support and to boost her courage. Erica gave a head nod and a grin that fueled the battery in Darlene's back.

"I ain't Big Wanda. Shit ain't gonna go down like that!" she spat. "I'll pay your hundred hotel fee after we done with this little piggy." Darlene's words were semi-slurred.

Starr looked over at Kathy, whose eyes were a tearing waterfall. Her pupils were dilating as if the high was beginning to take a toll on her. Starr leaned against the door and folded her arms, trying to figure out what punishment would be best for the two disrespectful fiends.

"Last chance to leave," Starr calmly remarked.

Just then, the remainder of the Double Gs came spilling into the cell one by one. Neither Darlene or Erica showed fear or stood down.

"Let me finish these li'l dumb bitches!" one of the Double Gs chimed. She was brandishing a jailhouse-made knife.

"No, let them go," Starr ordered. She pushed the closest Double Gs member to the side so a path could be made for the two fiends. She then gestured her hand to guide the two fiends out of her cell. Both women stood their position.

"Okay cool!" Starr's word was final. They were also stern enough to cause the two fiends to reconsider. Out of nowhere, Darlene stormed out of the cell followed by Erica.

"What the fuck happened while I was gone?" Starr barked as soon as the two fiends were gone.

All the Double Gs knew it was better to not say anything at all than to offer excuses or explanations. They all shrugged in unison. Starr shook her head. She knew she couldn't be mad at them. They were her sisters and Kathy wasn't, which meant Kathy was not their responsibility; Starr was. "Don't worry. This won't ever happen again. I promise," Starr assured Kathy. "You'll be straight until you're free, and when you get out, I got you," she ended.

Kathy heard everything Starr said, but nothing registered. The adrenaline rush, mixed with the drug's effects, had taken over her mind. Starr laid her head in her lap and stroked her hair until she fell asleep.

Two of the Double Gs bikers came upstairs to see what was up. "You want me to handle it?" one of the Double Gs asked.

"Nah, I got this. Trust me. We all should be out of here within the next week or so. I need to make sure nobody fucks with her when we're gone."

Starr had taken a serious liking to Kathy in such a short time. She was young, fragile, and innocent, which made her easily corruptible. Margaret's manipulation had landed her into federal prison. She knew hers would make her see life from a different perspective. Starr hated when the weak were preyed upon, and even more so she despised being tested. Besides, she had her own plans for Kathy.

About twenty minutes later Kathy woke up with her head still in Starr's lap, feeling like her brain had been frozen and on fire at the same time. For most people, cocaine kept them awake. But for Kathy, and all of the mental trauma she had been through during the past few days, it was all she needed to pass out. Her nose began dripping as she lifted her head. She was so embarrassed that she couldn't look Starr in her face as her face turned bright red.

"Drink a lot of water. Flush that garbage out of your system, and let that be an important lesson why to never do drugs," Starr stated with a motherly love as she stood up. Kathy didn't know how to respond. She had such an awful taste in her mouth. She slowly strolled over to the sink. Before she could attempt to brush her teeth she started throwing up in the toilet.

"That's one way to do it," Starr informed her, knowing Kathy would be fine. Kathy made her way back onto her feet, still feeling woozy. Kathy brushed her teeth and walked back over to the bed. Starr sat back down beside her.

"Thank you, for everything. I don't know what I would've done without you. I feel like I need to repay you for—"

"Nonsense," Starr interrupted, cutting her short. "I don't need anything from you. Just stay out of trouble. You're quite a handful," Starr playfully declared while softly mushing Kathy's head. Kathy's face lit up with a huge smile.

"I'd like to know more," she said as she swiftly touched the heels of her feet into her thighs to sit Indian style, with her elbows poled into her lap, and her hands under her chin.

"More what?" Starr asked with a raised eyebrow.

"About, you know, the organization. What do I have to do to become one of you?" she asked in a timid manner. "How do I become involved?"

Starr pondered whether she should tell her yet. She figured with all that Kathy had experienced in a short period of time, now would be as perfect a time as any. She leaned in to meet Kathy face to face. With the coldest eyes, Starr replied, "Okay, but this stays between us."

Chapter 30

Queen Fem sat at her kitchen table alone, sipping her morning latte. The headline along with the image on the front page of the newspaper her butler had just retrieved from the front door steps of her mini-mansion stared up at her. The statement DOUBLE TROUBLE FOR ALLEGED DOUBLE GS LEADER didn't sit well with her. It wasn't that she had a problem with the media naming somebody other than herself as the leader of the Double Gs. Her issue was the fact that the Double Gs were being publicly mentioned in the media.

Since she had launched and handpicked every Double G over twenty-five years ago when she was still actively involved with her organization, not once did she or any of the members bring such attention to them. She had managed to go undetected and evade the authorities by flying under their radar and making sure her members followed suit. She had also managed to transform herself into the infamous and mysterious Queen Fem without anyone making the connection between her monarch and her birth name of Carlita Banks.

She didn't even bother to open the paper up and read what she had already known. Thanks to her inside connect, she knew the moment they had arrested, released, and rearrested Starr. This was the first time in the history of the Double Gs that so much heat came their way, and Queen Fem did not like it. She had expressed to Starr on many occasions and warned her about her methods and measures when putting their victims in compromising positions that would put them in the "G" Files. She shook her head in disgust as she recalled the first video Starr had ever sent her. The strap-on addition to their extortion and blackmailing methods were too extreme for Queen Fem's taste, but she still allowed Starr to handle things the way she felt fit.

Not only was Starrshma Fields her protégé, she was also the daughter Queen Fem never had, which made it hard to tell her no since the day she laid eyes on her. The maternal side of her hated the fact that she couldn't intervene and help Starr. She knew she had to sit back and let things play out the way they were going to turn out and hope it went in Starr's favor.

She was more concerned about the effect the new attention and Starr's possible imprisonment may have on the Double Gs. *It's my own fault,* she told herself. She had spoiled Starr and allowed her to turn into the ruthless monster and limelight leader she had become; the sodomies, the killings, the partying among other things. But when she was first diagnosed with cancer, she knew Starr was the only member worthy and capable of ruling the organization with an iron fist. She both loved and respected Starr with all of her being, but she was pissed with her behind the back-to-back trouble she had managed to get herself in.

What does this mean for the Double Gs? Queen pondered. She wondered if would she have to resurface in order to keep the Double Gs intact while Starr was away, if that became the case, or whether she could appoint a temporary successor in Starr's absence. The thought frustrated her.

Queen Fem's thoughts were interrupted by the voice of her driver. "It's almost time for your chemo appointment, ma'am," the driver announced.

Queen Fem took a sip of her latte. "Thank you, Jane. I'll be to the car shortly."

The driver, Jane, nodded and excused herself from the kitchen.

Queen Fem covered her face with her hand and closed her eyes. *Think, Carlita,* she told herself. As the real boss of the Double Gs she knew she could only hope for the best for Starr, but prepare for the worst, for the sake of the Double Gs. A few other options and thoughts danced through her mind, but there was only one that really stood out, outside of her having to come out of seclusion. Queen Fem opened her eyes. The more she played with the idea the more it seemed most logical to her. She knew she'd have to toss it around some more in her mind, but she was almost certain it would be the right option if she was not up for exposing herself to the rest of the Double Gs.

With that being her thought, Queen Fem stood and placed her coffee cup in the sink. She then exited the kitchen and headed to her awaiting car outside of her home.

Chapter 31

Freeze answered his BMW 7 Series Bluetooth as he cruised down Flamingo Drive. Had it not been for who the caller was, he would have ignored the call and continued vibin' out to the Yo Gotti track as he navigated his way toward the casino.

"Yeah, what's poppin'?"

"Everything's straight on this end," Esco's words blared through the car speakers. "Just callin' to update you."

"Talk to me," Freeze shot back.

"That bitch from the club fuckin' with Prime heavy," Esco informed, referring to Monica. "I followed her to ol' dude crib a few times. I peeped one of his little soldiers watching one of the other chicks you wanted me to keep tabs on," he added, referring to Felicia. "I dunno what that's all about, though. But all them bitches was up in Treasure's a few nights ago ballin' out, poppin' bottles and shit." Esco played it back to Freeze the way it was told to him.

"Word? I thought it was over for that spot." Freeze's surprise was evident.

"Yeah, that's what I thought. That's why it sounds strange to me when I heard it. That's why I'm bringin' it to you," Esco said as a matter of fact.

Freeze pondered the news. There was no doubt in his mind that there was a reason behind the Double Gs being up in Treasures. "Yeah, shit do sound suspect," he agreed. "Stay on top of that and stay on them broads, too," Freeze spoke with emphasis in his tone.

"On it," Esco assured him.

"I know, homie," Freeze replied with admiration in his tone. "But, yo, let me get up off this phone, though. I'm about to go tear their ass up on this craps table right quick," Freeze announced.

Laughter could be heard on Esco's end. "You and them dice, bruh."

"Life's a gamble." Freeze's tone was serious.

"It sure is," Esco agreed. "Good luck, big homie," he offered before disconnecting.

Freeze increased the volume of his stereo system as he veered off into the direction of Bally's casino. The words "I am the struggle/ I am the hustle/I am the city," from Yo Gotti's "I Am" track filled the car's interior as Freeze replayed the information Esco had just given him. He had learned the hard way not to underestimate the Double Gs. They had made him a believer in the worst way, which was why he knew he wouldn't be able to rest until he got revenge.

Freeze tried to clear his mind. *What are these bitches up to now?* he wondered as he pulled into the casino's valet.

Chapter 32

Katherine States had been a computer wizard since she was barely even ten. She had gotten her first computer only the year before. It was a gift from her father, who was one of IBM's top technical engineers for eighteen years as a software designer/data analyst. Out of their three children, Kathy was the youngest of the family, ten whole years behind her twin brother and sister, who were both off to college at the time.

As a little girl, Kathy wasn't the type to ask questions. She'd much rather figure things out. So when she got her laptop on her ninth birthday, she sat in front of it all day and night until she understood the concept of having control over such a vast information center at her tiny fingertips. Once she discovered the unimaginable amounts of possibilities, she looked at the computer screen as a portal window to a new world. One where she could go anywhere she wanted, without ever moving.

She began to understand why her parents not only ignored her, but each other also. They would sit in front of their computer screens all day at work, and come home and do the same in separate home offices until late at night. That's when Kathy would sneak out of her room and hack into her parents' computers to see what they were up to. Her parents quickly caught on to their youngest daughter's mischievous ways and they both installed locked, coded passwords into their systems. It became a challenge for Kathy, one she found even more interesting.

Since she was always daddy's little girl, she cracked her father's code first, which was her birth date backward. Her mother's was much harder. It took almost two months of sneaking through the house in the middle of the night to find out that the code was the exact date that her parents had first made love, which was private information she retrieved from her mother's hidden diary.

Kathy's parents caught on quick. They both had been security breached by their beloved little angel. So they started changing their codes on the first of every month, using random mathematical equations. Some months were skipped by Kathy because they were just too hard. Others were cracked within a week. It became an addiction. Like a drug addict, her tolerance got higher and higher. She would come straight home from school, breeze through her homework, and then shuffle through all three computers before her parents got home.

Her mother's computer always held much more exciting information. Ironically, her mother was actually designing firewalls for security systems of all sorts. Kathy learned the step-by-step process of that on her own. The most intriguing thing she learned was that no data in a computer's mainframe was ever really lost or locked forever. Everything that was done could be retraced and undone. All you had to do was start backward and retrace the fingerprints.

By the time Kathy was sixteen, she followed in her mother's path and started to write her own software. Her unique skills got her a scholarship offered by many schools and universities, but she chose UNLV, only because her best friend Margaret was attending. Margaret was actually her only friend growing up. Being an obese teen prevented Kathy from winning any popularity contests, so if she wasn't hanging with Margaret she had her face buried in her laptop. Kathy relayed her rough childhood of being teased, bullied, and abused as a young girl. The two stayed

up trading stories for most of the entire night. The last
thing either of them remembered was the early morning
sun rising, shining right through the thin slot of window
glass that they could barely even see out of. They were
both so tired that neither of them woke up for breakfast.

Kathy was a long way from her college days when she
woke up 7:00 a.m. to the sound of her cell door unexpect-
edly being buzzed. Starr hopped up in a defensive mode,
but she noticed it wasn't an intruder alert; it was a female
guard.

"States! Get dressed. Court!" the guard announced
before stepping back off.

Kathy sat up rubbing her eyes, confused. She had no
knowledge of any court date for the day. She hoped that
it was another bail hearing because, up until that point,
both her and Margaret's parents decided not to bail
their daughters out, as a lesson. Starr secretly thought of
bailing Kathy out on her own, but she decided to let fate
play out.

Starr looked down at Kathy from her top bunk. She
watched her brush her teeth and fix her hair. In just
a short period of time, overnight, Kathy had become
like a daughter to Starr. To Starr, Kathy had a lot of
potential, as did most of the Double Gs members who
were personally selected.

After Kathy felt she was ready, she started to go out
the door but quickly turned back around, climbed up
on top of her bed, and gave Starr a big hug and planted
a kiss on her cheek. She then rushed back out after
hearing her name being called on the intercom. Starr
just shook her head. *She as green as a pool table carpet,*
she concluded.

Right after a skipped lunch, Starr was awakened
by her own name being called. It was another visit.
She was sure that it wasn't Diamond. She got up and
headed for the shower.

Once again, Starr was escorted to the visiting room floor where she saw Monica looking even better than the day prior. She didn't hesitate to make her way over to her. This time she wrapped her arms around Monica and boldly palmed her ass. Monica was caught by surprise but embraced Starr's touch. The feeling actually felt natural to her. She wondered if she was ever really acting in the first place, or if she was just finally embracing who she really was.

The two beautiful women sat down across from each other, held hands, and never let go.

"It's real good to see you again," Starr revealed.

"I had a dream about you last night," Monica flirtatiously retorted.

Starr blushed. "Oh, yeah?"

"Yes."

"Don't tell me now; wait until I get out," Starr retorted.

Monica nodded in agreement.

"So what's new? I know you didn't come up here to tell me you dreamed about me."

It was Monica's turn to blush. "No. Everything's fine. Diamond got the Spalding trial. Felicia got the bartending gig. Bubbles sends her regards and says to tell you the twins are Double Gs wholeheartedly. She said they almost started a war with the Spalding brothers." Monica laughed, remembering the story Bubbles had told her.

"What about you?" Starr asked.

"Me? I'm good." Monica smiled for a second time. "I'm taking it upon myself to hold you down. You need anything?"

"Right now, about ten minutes alone with you," Starr seriously joked in a seductive tone.

"I'm confident we could get it all done in five," Monica slyly responded.

As much as Starr was loving the verbal flirting match, she needed to get serious for at least a few minutes. "So, is everything in order for the mission I gave you?"

Monica's eyelids dropped low. She caught on to her own ill body language and quickly jumped back into character. "Yeah. The stage is all set. You sure you wanna?"

Starr's eyes turned cold. She hated being second-guessed.

Monica picked up on it and cleaned it up. "Don't worry. Consider it done."

"That's what I want to hear," Starr said. "Oh! There's just one other thing. When you come see me tomorrow, I need you to bring me something. It may seem light, but it's important to me."

"No problem," Monica assured her.

The visit had come to an end. Starr stood and pulled Monica in by the waist. Monica gazed into her eyes. She saw it coming and made no attempts to stop it. Starr leaned in and gave Monica a passionate and deep kiss. "See you later." Starr broke the lip lock and smiled. She walked off and left Monica speechless.

When she returned to the pod from her visit, Starr went straight to her cell. She was surprised to see Kathy back from court so early. She was balled up in the corner of her bunk. Starr could hear her crying through sniffles.

"What's up, Kat?" Starr asked with concern. In the short period of time she had known Kathy, she felt like a mother figure despite never having children of her own.

Kathy rolled over, wiping her face. Starr noticed she had a set of documents clenched in her hand. *Now what?* Starr wondered.

Kathy was too distraught to talk. She simply handed Starr the papers and used both of her hands to momentarily dry up her face, which wasn't working due to the overflowing stream of tears. "My life is ruined," she managed to sob.

Starr studied the cover page. The bold-print letters said it all. "Superseding indictment." Starr read through the contents and didn't like what she was seeing. It became clear that the reason Kathy and Margaret were separated was because Margaret had rolled over on Kathy in exchange for immunity. At first, the FBI only had the most recent crimes that they had committed, dating back during the last six months. Margaret led them in the right direction to dig up the buried tracks that uncovered what they would've never found. The same stuff she had forced Kathy to do. Now, Margaret has used it all to her personal advantage. Kathy went from facing twenty-six months to seventy-two months, which seemed like a lifetime to someone who never saw an inside of a jail before.

Starr was instantly infuriated. She crumbled up the pages in her fists. The one thing she couldn't stand was a snitch. It was because of an informant that she herself had managed to visit a jail cell not once, but twice in one week. "Where's that li'l bitch at now?" she questioned Kathy.

"She's over in her unit. They brought us back separately," Kathy sobbed.

"Don't worry. She won't get away with this," Starr vowed.

Starr's words made Kathy feel a little better. For some reason, she believed every word that she had just heard. There was something about Starr that made Kathy feel safe. Kathy didn't know how to feel about what she realized she was feeling for Starr. Starr made her feel protected and cared for, and while she wasn't comfortable with the way she felt, she was falling for Starr.

Kathy had been having explicit dreams and thoughts of her and Starr. Looking into her eyes, Kathy replayed in her mind the last dream she'd had of the two of them. In her mind, they weren't in prison; they were somewhere beautiful and far away from their current surroundings.

She daydreamed of Starr clad in a leopard-print thong and six-inch stilettos, carrying a tray of whipped cream and strawberries: her favorite. Starr approached her and fiercely removed her top and bra almost in one sweep. She began sucking on Kathy's already rock-hard nipples, before kissing her thighs softly and passionately. All while plunging a finger in and out of her dripping wet pussy, until she creamed all over herself. "Wow!" she mouthed to herself. That got her so hot that she had to get up and take off her sweatshirt as she continued to think about Starr. *I wish Starr saw me as more than just a new friend.*

Kathy touched herself on the low, careful not to let Starr or anyone else see, as her mind drifted off into more thoughts of Starr. She was afraid she would lose Starr as a friend and completely ruin her chances of being a member of the Double Gs, if she told her just how badly she wanted her. Still, she was determined that she was gonna get with Starr one day. Although Kathy hadn't told Starr yet, she was already anticipating being a part of her circle, no matter what it took.

Chapter 33

Diamond made a grand entrance, looking stunning as ever. She removed her shades and strutted down the aisle to her awaiting table of clients. Linda and Victoria paid her no mind. They both knew Diamond Morgan was trying to intimidate them. It wasn't until the judge was on the bench, and a witness was on the stand, that they even acknowledged that she was in the courtroom. They each had their A-game faces on today.

Throughout the previous day, Linda McCarthy had a hard time during the jury selection screening. She didn't know who to trust. She had firsthand knowledge of how good the Double Gs were at infiltrating. So, swaying a jury's verdict would be as simple as an NBA referee calling a hard foul in a playoff game. All these years she had no clue Diamond Morgan was even associated with, involved with, or one of them. It made things a lot more clear to her now.

She and Victoria pulled up every one of Diamond's prior cases, and with her newfound knowledge it all added up and made sense. All of the cops and witnesses had changed their statements, not shown up, or mysteriously disappeared . The same with the jurors. But there was no way to know for sure. Her gut was very untrusting with this particular case.

The genders of the jurors were split. Six women, six men, and a female alternate juror in case she had to fill in. Linda wondered if any of the females were one of or affiliated with the Double Gs. She also questioned whether any of the males on the jury were under their spell as well. There was absolutely no way to tell. The jury pool's depth wasn't that strong. Most of them were too young for Linda's liking. She wanted an elderly crowd, which blatantly would've gone against the Spaldings' constitutional rights of being tried by a jury of their peers. As the head U.S. Attorney of all America, this was the first time Linda McCarthy felt like the underdog.

Everyone rose to their feet as Judge Stewart exited her chambers and claimed her seat on the throne of justice. The trial was finally about to begin. The deputy was sent to call the jury in to fill the wooden panel. All thirteen of them sat in their chairs. Some looked frustrated as if they didn't want to be there. Others gave the impression that they couldn't wait to get started. Neither side was a good sign.

After the jury instructions were given, it was time for the opening arguments, which was a basic verbal introduction of the case, but more so a wordplay battle between the prosecutor and the defense lawyer. Being that defendants are always presumed innocent until proven guilty, it was the prosecutor's burden to strike first. Linda McCarthy and Victoria Stockford whispered between each other for a few seconds while reviewing notes. Linda then removed her reading glasses, stood up, adjusted her attire, and strutted over to the jury panel. Her heels planted themselves directly in front of them as she stared each of the thirteen jurors in their eyes all at once, with the seriousness of silence instigating the tone she was setting.

Diamond sat at her table with her five clients, her pen hovering over the yellow legal notepad, prepared to mark down any inconsistency, mistake, objection, key question, or flat-out deliberate lie she might encounter. From that point on the war had officially begun.

Linda spoke in a low, steadily stern voice, rotating eye contact among the jurors. She understood that, from this point on, no one else's opinions mattered other than the jury. Not the judge, not the witnesses, not the spectators, not the defendants, and certainly not Diamond's or her own.

"During this trial, you will hear the chilling testimonies of law enforcement officials, witnesses, and victims of the most audacious string of bank robberies this city has seen in decades," Linda McCarthy opened up with. "And as they bravely relive those unforgettably horrendous memories so that justice may be served, they will heroically walk you through them, step by step, painting the most vivid images for you. That is the job that they have come forward to do. And they are meeting the judicial system halfway. You ladies and gentlemen of the jury also have a job. The most important one, which is the rare opportunity to deliver that justice. Right now, as I stand here and speak on behalf of this court and all of America, it is up to you all, and no one else, to put murderers like the Spalding brothers away for life." She turned to face the Spalding brothers and she waved her hand down the row where they sat, to put a visual to her words.

"Banks are filled with nothing but honest, taxpaying citizens such as yourselves," she continued. "That means that it could've been any one of you there at the time of those brutal robberies. Any of you all could've been hostages with the barrels of huge submachine guns with names you couldn't even pronounce pointed at you, and maybe even your children. It could've been your sons or your daughters in any one of those banks at the time the Spalding brothers felt that they were above the law. For those innocent people who were there, it was a horrific nightmare." Linda McCarthy let her words marinate on the jury before she continued.

"Along with the testimonies, indisputable evidence will be presented to you. You may examine any specific piece of it for as often and as long as you would like. It is your right. The court believes we have enough evidence stacked to mark this what we call an open and shut case. During the review of this evidence and witnesses testimony, I leave you with the key element of determining a verdict for this case. A reminder. A reminder that in order to convict these defendants, all it takes to serve justice on a silver platter is the fact that all it has to be is more than likely that the Spalding brothers committed these heinous acts. That's all it takes to prove that it was indeed these men who walked into our banks, took some of our taxpayers' money, and killed our fellow citizens in cold blood. And, ladies and gentlemen, when I say 'our' that's exactly what I mean. Not as a prosecutor, but as a taxpaying citizen, who could've also been in one of those banks."

Linda McCarthy thought about thanking the jurors for their time as an extended ending, but she didn't want to overdo it. She wanted to purposely leave the imprint that what the jurors were being asked to do by her was their duty, not a favor. She turned on her heels and strolled away. She took a quick glance over at Diamond, who paid her no mind. Linda McCarthy noticed she had been writing nonstop since her opening argument. She sat next to Victoria Stockford and exhaled lightly. She then leaned over to her partner. "How'd I sound?"

Victoria Stockford's smile was all the confirmation Linda McCarthy needed. She knew it wasn't going to be an easy case, but at least she knew she was off to a great start.

Chapter 34

The entire weekend was profitless. Sammy woke up, feeling the pain of spending more than he made. With Club Panties out of order, people were finding other places to party instead of Club Treasures. Had it not been for the fifteen grand the Double Gs had spent one night last week, he would have had to have dip into monies he couldn't afford to touch. Even the high-class dancers who worked for him were abandoning ship due to how slow it was.

Sammy was all out of options, with the exception of one. He was hoping it didn't have to come to this. He had already regretted his initial decision. It was the cause of his recent drought. Now, he was ready to do anything to get his establishment back up and running.

Sammy crawled out of his bed and retrieved his phone from his phone clip attached to his Ferragamo belt. Before pulling up the number he intended to call, he had a mental talk with himself. *You sure about this?* He was still battling with the decision.

"Fuck it!" he yelled out. He refused to go through another weekend like he just had. He scrolled through his contacts and pulled up the number he had stored in his phone for years, but had never used. As he pres-sed the call button, he thought about the benefit in the antic-ipated conversation he expected to have with the caller. Not once did he think about the part he had played and the fact that he had brought his situation on himself behind it.

Chapter 35

Felicia had no interest in reading about Officer Blake, especially when she knew the details firsthand. She skipped past that section of the newspaper and went straight to the puzzles to pass the time as she sat in her rental car's driver seat awaiting Monica to exit her apartment.

Felicia was no stranger to following orders, especially when given by two separate people. Originally, she had been following Monica under Starr's orders, when she had disappeared with Prime. Felicia was an expert tail and knew she couldn't successfully follow them that night without being made. Prime's driving was too skillful. He seemed to know all of the tricks to making a tracking car stand out. She had kept a watchful eye on Monica, per Diamond's request, being that she was temporarily in charge while Starr was locked down. She reported all of Monica's movements to Diamond.

It was the fifth day in a row that Felicia had followed Monica. The first few days she had tailed her all of the way to and back from the jail. She knew Monica was coming right back out because her car was still running. Felicia was undecided on whether she would hold back the information about Monica visiting Starr back to back. The last thing she wanted to do was alarm Diamond and add to her suspicion. She knew Diamond knew something based on the tapes she had watched. Felicia just didn't know exactly what she knew. She didn't want to find herself caught up in a matrix and jeopardize her own position.

Felicia's thoughts were broken by the sight of Monica. Monica emerged from the co-op building's lobby, suspiciously looking both ways before getting back in her car. Felicia rose up and put her car back in drive. She was surprised to see that Monica didn't pull off. She was just sitting there. From down the block, behind her, she had a clear view through Monica's back window. She watched Monica answer her cell phone.

A second wave of minutes passed before Felicia heard the roaring of two motorcycles coming behind her. She quickly ducked down just in time before getting made by the two Double Gs. She recognized the twins bikes.

Felicia watched as Sparkle pulled up close to Monica's window and dug into her pocket. She slipped her something that Felicia couldn't make out. She just watched as the three girls laughed and joked for a few seconds; and then Sparkle and Glitter vanished up the block. Felicia rose up as Monica exited her car and reentered her building. She shortly returned after dropping whatever it was off in her apartment. She got back in her car and pulled off.

Felicia pulled off seconds later.

Chapter 36

Young Clips knew he was on to something big, but he never imagined it was this huge. He possessed detailed information that could change the game anytime he chose, but he continued to keep it to himself until he felt it was the right time. Initially, he was infatuated with Felicia, almost to the point of being considered a stalker. He had been following Felicia around nonstop for weeks, hoping to get her attention outside of her crew, to no avail. Slowly but surely he began to abandon the idea of ever having a chance with her. That's when he began to focus on gathering info that may be useful to Prime and their crew.

It got to the point where he started recording her events with his cell phone everywhere she went. He knew where almost all of the top Double Gs members lived, along with their daily routines and criminal activities by following Felicia. What started as pure puppy love for Clips turned into an investigation and the biggest business opportunity anyone in the city would ever come close to. Dealing with any of the Double Gs members, secrets were hard to unveil. It was starting to seem like each of them had some. Not just from the rest of the world, but from each other. This was the chance to singlehandedly beat the Double Gs at their own game. "Blackmail." He craved more data and he knew it would come. The snowball effect was getting bigger. There was no way it could stop rolling and growing now. Soon, he planned to be the avalanche to end it all.

Clips pulled off after Felicia, following while keeping a safe distance. Unbeknownst to him, Clips also had an unwanted guest on his tail.

It was the easiest money Smoke had ever made. He jumped at the opportunity when Prime offered him $250 a day to follow Clips. Prime knew Clips wasn't expecting it. Smoke didn't have much knowledge of the Double Gs besides the street rumors and news reports, nor did he care. Smoke was only seventeen years old. He was a young gun-slinging heavy weed smoker with a short fuse. With the free money he was getting, he could indulge in the things he loved the most, getting high and buying the latest sneakers, without dipping into his regular hustling money.

He shadowed Clips everywhere he went. As he followed him, Smoke concluded that Clips was a stalker at first. But after witnessing what Clips had been witnessing himself, he realized Clips was actually on to something. Smoke started paying closer attention. When he made his updated reports to Prime, he withheld one piece of info, stacking his own deck. He planned to wait it out and see how he could benefit from what he knew to be valuable information.

Clips veered off onto the exit as he followed Felicia, who was following Monica. Smoke was trailing at a safe distance. Once he saw the blinker of Clips's whip, he sped up. He got off on the same exit as the other three cars. *Where are we headed today?* Smoke thought as he exited the highway.

Monica headed up Interstate 15 and got off on a deserted exit that led to a gated private airplane hangar. It was a huge aluminum garage that sat in the middle of nowhere. Monica ignored the No Trespassing sign and drove straight through the open field, parking on the side of the building. It took a few minutes before she got out. When she did, those secretly watching her from afar noticed that she had put on some sort of disguise. She had on a long blond wig, big, dark shades, and a ton of makeup. A silk scarf hung over her face and down the sides of her face. She pulled her trench coat closed as she quickly strutted into the wide-open garage.

Aside from a few of the private planes that hovered in the sky, four of them were parked in the garage side by side. Monica passed each of the two passenger planes that resembled the modern air-fighter craft from the old days, or much like the ones the Wright brothers were famous for using. One of them looked like an old two-seater war plane. Monica's eyes scanned for any sign of a gun attached.

"What can I do for you, young lady?" a country accent echoed, startling Monica. Up until that point, there hadn't been any signs of human presence. She looked around and saw an older white man ducking from under the third craft carrier from the front. He was wiping his fingers off with an oily towel, which seemed to be making things worse. He reached over to shake Monica's hand.

She stared at it rudely, with disgust, and ignored the formal gesture. Instead, she got right down to business. "Are you Jake Stolkoff?" she asked.

Jake retracted his hand and smiled, proudly revealing his decayed rows of teeth. "Yes. Yes, I am. What can I do you for?" he asked.

Monica remained stern. She reached into her purse, pulled out $1,500, a map with a marked pinpointed location, and a note with a time stamped on it. Jake took everything and reviewed the contents. "Lady, are you serious?" he asked.

Monica frowned at him, starting to walk away.

"This is way too much," Jake declared as he counted the hundred dollar bills.

"Keep the change. Just make sure you're there at the exact location at the exact time," she yelled without looking back.

For Jake, it seemed to be the strangest overpaid request that he had ever gotten in his line of business. But what did he care? He was $1,500 richer, for a $350 job.

"Damn, I miss that dick," Monica said to herself as she slipped back in her car. "Maybe I should call Black to meet up and get a little piece before going back to my day-to-day life as a member of the Double Gs."

Monica picked up her cell phone as she pulled out of the seemingly empty lot. The man who belonged to the deep, masculine voice that instantly soaked her panties answered on the first ring.

Before she could say a word, Black knew it was his baby. "Long time, no hear, Mon."

"I know. Look, no time to chat. Are you home alone?"

"Yes."

"Be there in fifteen." Monica hung up the phone, both sets of lips smiling as she pressed hard on the gas.

Monica thought back to the very first time she met Black, which was also the first time she had slept with him. She couldn't help thinking back to the day Black changed her life forever.

There she was on the other side of town, working to complete an assignment for her journalism class. She was closing her car door when a fine young brother appeared out of nowhere and stood between the door and the car. For a minute Monica thought she was being robbed. Her heart raced while the rest of her body went numb.

"What's wrong, shawty? You too fine to look so sad."

Since he hadn't demanded her purse or forcefully snatched her out of the car, she figured that she was okay for the moment. *"Things just haven't gone the way I'd planned for them today, but thanks."* Something was telling Monica to leave as fast as she could, but her kitty was purring a different tune. The young man who stood before her was fine as hell. He was tall, with a smooth, dark chocolate complexion, deep-set dimples, and a charming smile comparable to that of Blair Underwood's.

"The homies around here call me Black. What's ya name?" He extended his hand and she slowly reached out and firmly shook it. His grip was strong, and Monica imagined his hands around her thick, round hips, guiding them as she slid up and down his shaft.

"I'm Monica."

"Monica. That's a sexy name for a sexy mama." Black was grinning, showing off his expensive grill.

"Thank you." Monica tried not to, but she couldn't help but blush. To her own surprise, she was feeling him.

"Yo, shawty . . ."

Monica cut her eyes at him, and he changed his tune. She hated being referred to as shawty, ma, and all that nonsense. Where she came from, people referred to each other by the names they were given at birth. She didn't know anyone with shawty or ma on their birth certificates.

"I mean, Ms. Monica, you wanna go cop some dinner? I'm kinda in the mood for some Red Lobster."

Monica couldn't believe he had asked her out to dinner. She was supposed to be meeting her boyfriend, Robert, in an hour for dinner at his place. Robert always made burnt hamburgers, and Monica was sick of them. Red Lobster sounded more pleasant; and, as if on cue, her *stomach growled, begging her to take Black up on his offer rather than subjecting it to Robert's main course.*

"Black, I have got to tell you that I do have a boyfriend." Honesty is the best policy, right?

"Monica, all I want is some dinner, and I figured you might want some too." *Even though he was acting tough on the outside, she could see that her having a boyfriend wasn't exactly what he wanted to hear. Of course, he wasn't going to tell her that.*

"I'm sorry for jumping to conclusions. Just let me call him and let him know that I'll be a little late."

Robert wasn't thrilled with the idea of Monica hanging out with Black, but it was just dinner, so he eventually gave in. She tried to feed herself the same line of bullshit, but judging by the throbbing in her panties, she knew that pleasure was right around the corner.

"You said you wanted to go to Red Lobster, right?"

"Yeah, ma, let's hit Red Lobster."

Monica didn't even check him on calling her ma. She was too busy watching his thick lips move. Damn, he sure is sexy. He was tall and muscular, and his cologne was intoxicating, rendering her tipsy off of pure lust.

Black cleared his throat, snapping her out of her daze. Why in the world was she thinking about how sexy this man looked and smelled? She already had a man, and Robert was nice enough. Robert also had a good job as a paralegal and was in law school. The only qualities Monica hated about him were that he was judgmental and egotistical, and he didn't have a clue what to do with the juicy, wet pussy that she put on him. He wasn't working with much in that department, and what little bit he had Robert didn't have a clue how to work it or work her.

"Monica, did you see the game last night? My fault; I guess I should have asked if you even like sports."

They shared platters of beer-battered shrimp and chips, and crab legs. It definitely beat the hell out of those hamburgers of Robert's. The more she and Black talked, the more she realized that they had a lot in common. "I love sports, especially football, and yes, I caught the game."

He smiled approvingly, and Monica was turned on the more they had in common. It was obvious that he was pleased to meet a woman who was into his favorite sport. It was also obvious that he was feeling her, even if he didn't want to admit it.

"I wasn't too impressed with my boys last night. I got mad love for them, but it was like they weren't even trying and they had home-field advantage."

Monica was thinking about how good his lips would taste against hers. Black was talking to her and his lips were moving, but she didn't hear a sound. She was in her own world and in her world they weren't at Red Lobster. In Monica's world, he was moaning in her ear and it was driving her crazy.

"Damn, boo, you taste so good."

He was licking and kissing her shoulders and neck, and all she could think was, *if you love that, just wait until you taste Kitty LaRue,* her pet name for her pussy.

"So you like that, huh?" she purred back at him just as her kitty was beginning to do some meowing of her own. "I think it's time that you meet my best friend, Kitty LaRue."

"Who's Kitty LaRue, shawty?" he asked, suckling her nipples, driving her to the point of madness.

She took his masculine hand and gently placed it on her love tunnel. "This is Kitty LaRue." She squirmed a little as he inserted his forefinger into her honey pot. His touch was magical, hence the nickname Mr. Magic Fingers. She loved his manual stimulation. Before she knew what had happened, he had all four of his magical fingers deep inside her pleasure zone, and his thumb was massaging her clitoris. He was urging her to lose all of her inhibitions and release all of her love juices on him. Her wish was his command.

"Let it go, boo. It's okay; just let it go." His face was a mask of pleasure, as if he knew that she had never felt so free to be herself. Before she knew it, she came all over his hand. Black slowly brought those magic fingers to his thick lips and licked them clean like a double scoop of ice cream on a waffle cone.

"Monica? Yo, earth to Monica." Black was laughing and licking his lips like he knew exactly what she was thinking.

"Umm, yeah, Black?" Even with her mocha-colored skin, she imagined it being beet red from sheer embarrassment. Monica felt moisture between her thick thighs, and she knew that she was so aroused by this man, a virtual stranger, that it was unreal. Monica had never had this reaction to any other man without him touching her first.

"What you thinking about, ma?" He looked at her and their eyes connected. She knew that she didn't have to say a word because he knew exactly what she wanted and needed.

Monica raised her hand to get the server's attention and she requested the check. As she was digging out her credit card, Black took her hand firmly, yet gently. "No, boo, I got it. I told you I got you. You didn't believe me?"

She didn't at first, but she was digging his take-charge attitude. Robert made a lot more money than she did, but he wouldn't have had a problem letting her pay. Lately, he had been forgetting his wallet at home. Monica was sure that he was doing it purposely.

"Shawty? You sure you wanna do this?" They were back at Monica's place, and she had just dimmed the lights and put on a slow jam CD. The look on his face seemed to be of genuine concern.

"As you can see, I'm a big girl; I can take it. Don't worry; I'll try not to get too attached. I understand if you have other women that you see. I'm not the jealous type." Truth was Monica did mind, because she was really feeling him, but if he wanted to play hard, she'd match his hardness.

"No, Monica, that's not what I mean. I mean, are you sure that you want to make love to a dude you just met? Especially since you got a man and all."

"Well . . ."

"I know he can't be doing you right if you're here with me. I mean, look at you." He stopped and took a deep breath and then looked Monica up and down. "You're smart and you sexy. What kinda dude don't want a girl like you on his arm? What kinda man wouldn't treat you like the queen you are?" Was it that obvious? Without even meeting Robert or seeing them together, he knew she wasn't happy.

"Black, you don't have to butter me up just to get me to sleep with you. I already want to sleep with you." She was forever the skeptic and never one to believe anything positive that someone said about her. Her self-esteem had been lowered over the years after being the butt of fat jokes from her peers.

"Look, I'm glad that you wanna do this, but I'm not trying to just 'butter' you up. I really like you, Monica." She opened her mouth to speak but he kissed her long and hard. The same way she imagined his dick to be. Long and hard! Finally, after what felt like an eternity, he let her up for air, and she felt like she was floating on air. His kiss was like a whirlwind of emotions, and

Monica was beginning to feel them all at once. All that was certain was that she had never felt that way before. She was on fire, and Black was the only man to extinguish that ravishing fire that blazed between her thick, rotund thighs.

"Black, make love to me." There wasn't a doubt in her mind that her crummy day was going to have a very happy ending.

"Mmm, that's what's up, shawty."

He scooped her up in his arms as if she only weighed 125 pounds instead of 235 pounds, and he effortlessly carried her straight to her bedroom as if he had been there before. When they reached the bed, he sat her down just as smoothly as he had picked her up, leaving her speechless.

"Ooh, Black," was all she could moan. He looked up at her and smiled, sliding one of her Gucci ankle boots off, kissing her toes through her thigh-high stockings, all while smoothly transitioning to her other foot, removing her shoe, and slipping her stockings off in one swoop.

Black then took her foot out of his mouth and removed that stocking with his teeth without ripping it. Brotha got moves! Monica thought.

"I know you got a man, boo, but can I have you just for tonight?"

Monica wished this nigga would stop bringing up Robert. She certainly wasn't thinking about Robert's ass. "Don't worry about him. I'm not." Those must have been just the words he needed to hear, because from that moment it was on and popping. He flipped her over onto her stomach, raised her skirt, and ripped her thongs off, in one swoop motion.

Then he said, "Roll over, baby," with a sexy huskiness in his voice. He was definitely turning her out, and he hadn't even played with the phat pussy yet.

Monica always felt like she had to take control in the bedroom, so she was happy being under his sexual command. In fact, it felt damn good. She rolled over to find that he had his pants and boxers off and was standing there looking so inviting in nothing but his Timberland boots, licking his luscious lips.

She was aching for his thug passion and Black knew it. He reached forward, pulling her skirt off; and she was getting wetter by the moment. Then he handed her a condom before she could even reach into her nightstand drawer. "Put this on me, baby girl." He was standing there holding his huge manhood that almost made her run away.

She had never had a man so endowed before, so she was excited, nervous, and scared. Her mind was telling her to run like hell, but her pussy cat was purring so loudly, begging her to stay. Of course her pussy won that fight. Thank God. She took a deep breath and began to place the condom on his manhood and roll it up to the base of his shaft.

"Naw, baby girl, put it on with yo' mouth."

Monica had never done this before, nor had she even heard of it, but it kind of turned her on. So, she took the condom off and placed the tip of it in her mouth. Slowly she inched it halfway up his manhood with her lips and tongue.

"Black, I can't go any farther with my mouth." Instantly she felt bad, like she wasn't pleasing him.

"Boo, it's cool. I never expected you to be able to go all the way up. This is twelve inches of steel. What I'm lovin' is the fact that you tried. That's sexy as hell, ma."

Feeling better about the situation, she placed her hand around his shaft and massaged the condom the rest of the way up his thick, pulsating manhood. It amazed her that putting the condom on him that way was so arousing. Very. She guessed that's what being grown and sexy, safely, really meant. He leaned forward and kissed her and she was loving the passionate way he kissed her.

She was so happy that she had stuffed her secrets into one of her Victoria's Secret bras that day, instead of her usual plain Jane bras. He was making her feel so desirable, so sexy, something she hadn't felt in a long time. She felt so good that she vowed to herself right then and there that she would always do whatever she had to do to always feel that way. Even if she had to do it all alone.

Black laid her gently on the bed, kissing her neck, shoulders, and then the tops of each of her breasts. Then he ran his hands across her thick belly, grabbing her love handles as he kissed his way down her thighs. She felt as if she had died and gone to heaven. All she knew was if she was dreaming, she never wanted to wake up.

He had driven Monica all the way to the edge of ecstasy and pulled her back, and he took her there again and again. She had never felt anything like that before, and she knew in her heart of hearts that she would be damned if she was going back to mediocre loving after that night. By the time he entered her with his long, thick manhood, all it took was a few slow strokes before she was thrown completely over the edge of eroticism. It was the most intense orgasm that she had ever experienced. Leaning forward, he huskily whispered in her ear, "I love this thickness on you, ma."

"I love the way you love this thickness, baby." Black made Monica feel like a sexual goddess. Like she was on top of the world and nothing or no one could ever stand in her way. The way he was doing her body told her that she could have anything she wanted, whenever she wanted it. What she wanted at that very moment was for him to go back down south and let

his mouth get acquainted with her hot pussy, aka Miss Kitty. He was kissing her pert and perky nipples, so she pushed down on his shoulders and started him on a path back down.

"Kiss me here," she instructed, pointing underneath her breasts. "Mmm, kiss me here, baby." Following directions to a T, he kissed her belly button. "Oh, Black, kiss me here," she moaned, spreading her pussy lips farther apart, massaging her clit.

"Say no more, ma." Monica's new perfect lover went downtown like she was his last meal and he intended to get every single drop. He wasn't like her ex, Savon. That man used to always lap at it like the pussy was a doggy dish and he was a malnourished bulldog! He certainly wasn't like Robert's no-skills-having self, using his damn teeth. It had gotten to the point that she never wanted Robert to touch her anymore, even before she met Black. After being under his hypnotic spell, she couldn't imagine anyone ever being a better lover than him.

He entered Monica, and she lost herself in their rhythm.

"Oh, Black! Oh, shit! Black!" She clawed his back as she came all over his latex-covered manhood, and she loved it. "Oh, Black, I'm sorry, baby, I hope I didn't hurt you."

Black stared her directly in the eyes and spoke softly. "Monica, it's okay, baby, that's what my back is here for, for you to claw at. I wanted to give you an orgasm like you've never experienced before, baby. You were bound to react some type of way."

Smiling, she looked down and noticed that he was still rock hard. All she could think was, dayum, as hung as he is, and he's still hard as a rock. Oh, my God, I'm falling in lust. *Monica knew that it wasn't love, not yet. She did know that she wanted him and only him to be her full-time lover.*

He pulled another condom out of his pants pocket, bent over, and kissed her on her forehead. "Be right back, sexy mama." Off to the bathroom he went, and damn, she couldn't help but say that she enjoyed the view of him going almost as much as she enjoyed viewing him cumming.

Monica awoke the next morning to the smell of coffee brewing, scrambled eggs, bacon, and French toast. She looked over at her nightstand at her favorite book, Office Affairs. She was feeling good, knowing that she had finally experienced mind-blowing sex and didn't just have to read about it. Experiencing afterglow thrilled her and sent chills down her spine. Smiling so hard that her cheeks started to hurt, she stretched as she headed to the shower. When she got there, she was surprised to find a brand new robe and towel set, along with a strawberry-champagne bubble bath gift set sitting on the shelf. Folded neatly on top of it was a note. He must have slipped out to the store down the street while she was sleeping. The note read:

> *My dearest Monica,*
> *As you sleep so peaceful and serene, I wanted to do something to thank you just for being you, and to start your day off with a smile.*
> *Mad Love,*
> *Black*

With him being there, her day couldn't help but to start off with a smile. She turned her multiple-head shower on full force. She made sure that she got it to the perfect temperature before stepping inside. Monica had been in the shower for maybe ten minutes or so and was about to step out when the room went dark. At first she thought that the power had gone out, but she knew that couldn't have been the case, because the water was still piping hot. Just the way she liked it. Then, she felt an arousing and masculine presence behind her, and once again her smile was as wide as a country mile.

"Mmm, you taste so sweet in the morning." Black slowly kissed her down her neck, shoulders, and back.

Monica reached down and grabbed his fully aroused manhood. "And you feel so amazing in the morning." He was harder than twelve boulders. Monica knew in her heart that he wanted to make love to her, and she couldn't wait for him to verbalize his desires.

"How about a little dessert before breakfast?"

She loved the creative way he used his words. It turned her on, big time. "I thought you'd never ask." Still holding on to his tool, she turned around and wrapped her leg around his waist. "Mmm, damn, Black, you sure do know how to make a sista feel sexy in the morning."

He smiled and proceeded to go down and taste her wet, creamy core. Monica stopped him and said, "No, baby, I'm a little hungrier than I thought. You mind if I have some sausage for breakfast?" With that she slid down the length of his sexy body and welcomed him into her warm, eager mouth.

In a matter of weeks, Black and Monica fell head over heels in love, and she knew that he was the man her heart desired. It was time for her to let Robert go, not that she was spending much time with him anyway. After being introduced to Black's loving, she wouldn't even allow Robert to sniff her sweet pussy.

Monica made it her business to find something to argue about every time he called, and she always made excuses as to why she wouldn't go to dinner with him. He deserved to know the truth, and she and Black deserved to have an exclusive relationship, so she invited Robert over for dinner: the last supper.

"Monica, the spaghetti is good. I love when you bake it and add pepperoni on top of the cheese."

She nodded and took a sip of her iced tea.

"But, it could use a little more seasoning." He was always overly critical and had to find the bad in every single thing. If he made it to heaven, he'd be the bastard trying to tell God how to improve eternity.

She'd had more than a belly full of him, so she decided to hurry the evening along and send him on his way. Monica had already had his bag with the few items he'd left at her place packed and ready to go.

"Robert, I met someone else." She'd thought that she wouldn't be able to look him in the eyes when she told him but, surprisingly, she stared straight into his face with no shame.

He chewed his garlic bread slowly while staring at her and waiting for more.

"I'm in love, Robert, and it's not with you. I didn't mean for it to happen, but it did and I don't want to see you anymore." Monica wasn't about to say that she was sorry because she wasn't sorry for falling in love with Black.

Robert laid his fork down and folded his hands together on the table. "Is it the guy you had dinner with about six weeks ago? The guy you said you were writing your article on?"

Monica nodded affirmatively. "His name is Black, and we connected that night over dinner. We've been seeing each other every day since that night, and I realize it's not fair to you, him, or myself for me to continue seeing you."

"So, how long have you been screwing him?" he calmly asked while bringing the glass of iced tea to his thin lips.

"Does it really matter how long? Didn't you hear what I said, Robert? I'm in love with him, and I don't want to see you anymore." Maybe she owed him more of an explanation but the bottom line was not going to change. She wanted nothing more to do with Robert.

"I guess it doesn't matter." He rose from his chair. *"Thanks for dinner and have a nice life, Monica."*

She was baffled by his calmness but it didn't really matter one way or another. She just wanted him out of her life, so she hurried to the other room and retrieved his bag while he waited by the door.

"I think I packed everything but, if not, I'll use a courier service to deliver anything else I may find," Monica offered while handing him his bag.

"You know, Monica, I should have known a spoiled, fat bitch like yourself wouldn't know how to appreciate a good man such as myself." He sneered.

"Excuse me?" Monica asked, ready to slap fire from his face.

"Oh, you heard me. It's stupid black heifers like you who make good black men go out and marry white women. Then you sit on your fat asses crying with your girlfriends over ice cream and cake about how all the good black men are switching out."

Monica raised her hand, drew back, and slapped spit from his mouth. When he opened his mouth to speak, she backhanded him with the same hand. If she'd had a gun, she probably would have shot Robert Montford in cold blood and spit on his corpse. How dare he disrespect her in her own home? He had a right to be angry, but he had no right to disrespect her.

"When that thug starts beating your butt, don't call me," he hissed between clenched teeth. *"Call Jenny Craig and see if she can recommend a diet for fat and stupid chicks."*

She'd balled up her fist to punch him square in his wide nose but, instead of hitting him, she laughed. "Robert, if I was on fire, I wouldn't call you to spit on me. I'd rather burn up than have anything to do with you." Monica walked so close to him that she was practically standing on his feet. "Now, if you don't get the hell out my house, I'll call Black over here to kick your ass."

"Screw you, Monica!" Robert yelled over his shoulder as he walked hurriedly toward his silver Audi.

"Maybe if you'd known how none of this would have happened!" She slammed the door and called Black to come over. Her anger had her aroused, or maybe it was because she was finally free from Robert's dumb ass. But either way she was worked up and ready to go.

"What's up?" he answered on the first ring.

"I hope you are, but if you're not I know how to get you there."

"I'll be there in ten minutes. I want you naked and down on all fours with that big, juicy booty up in the air waiting on daddy!"

Monica squealed in delight as she flipped the phone closed and rushed to the bathroom to freshen up. One man's junk was surely another man's treasure.

Can a man change his lifestyle? The answer is a resounding yes, if he chooses to do so. Black and Monica were married after two years of dating. Her husband proved to be quite smart. In fact, he had taken business and marketing classes at a community college. His expensive grill was nothing more than a removable plate, and his hard exterior was all about having to be tough in the neighborhood where he'd grown up. He actually possessed business savvy that matched his street wit.

Six years after their first encounter, Monica's husband was now the CEO of his own advertising company, and she couldn't have been more proud of him. He took care of business at the office and still worked his magic at home. She missed being at home with him every day, but that was the life they both chose when she joined the ranks as an FBI agent.

Chapter 37

Diamond hoped the jury didn't fall for U.S. Attorney Linda McCarthy's false humbleness, along with her national anthem "Star-Spangled Banner" speech. In case they did, Diamond already had every intention of making sure they didn't. Going after the DA was one of the best parts about being a lawyer, let Diamond tell it. They had the opportunity to flip everything the prosecutor previously said.

Diamond stood up from her seat after reviewing her jotted notes. When she finally approached the jury panel, she spoke with the aggression of an antagonist.

"Ladies and gentlemen of the jury, in many ways I do agree with prosecutor McCarthy. But in more ways, I don't. And here's why you shouldn't either. Although I respect her patriotic approach, I highly disagree with her blatant deception."

The jury seemed staggered by the audacious callout. But it woke them up from the bore of things. Diamond had sensed the deflated state that Linda had left them in. Now that she had been granted the effect that she was looking for, she continued.

"According to her, my clients don't deserve a fair trial. Her order to you all was to convict them. She never once said to you all to use logic, or even your own opinion. She never explained that the testimony you hear might be contradicting or just simply not enough. She never expressed that the so-called evidence is just clues to putting together the story of what really happened, which is why we're here today. To figure out what really happened." Diamond paused. She took a moment to let her opening remarks marinate in the minds of the jurors, and then added, "Together."

Linda McCarthy couldn't help but let out a chuckle. Diamond caught it but didn't flinch or show any indication that she had heard her.

"This isn't my side against her side," she continued. "No," she boomed. "We are all here in search of the truth. Even my clients. They are here today on their own free will. If they were in fact as vicious as the prosecution claims, then they would've left the bail money behind and run. No, we are all representing justice today. We are all a part of the court. And we will get to the bottom of things. Right now, my clients are innocent. So they, too, are taxpaying citizens."

Diamond then spun around and directed her attention to Linda McCarthy. "Mrs. McCarthy also manipulatively informs you all that if you feel that just one of my clients is likely to have done these crimes by 50.1 percent of your opinion, then they're all guilty. Wrong! However, you are burdened by the greater weight of the evidence. So please, by all means, listen to the testimony. I'm quite positive they will explain that some terrible things have happened. I am certain that they will not be able to pinpoint my clients as the ones responsible. But still, I warn you. Be very careful. A lot of victims seek closure. So as long as someone is being blamed or in custody, to get it all over with they want to believe that it's those people who should be held accountable. The same way with law enforcement, witnesses and, yes, even jurors.

"It's true. I am sure that all of your lives have been interrupted by this, and you are all eager to get it over with. And a guilty verdict always seems to be the quickest and easiest choice. But this is the part where I actually agree with Mrs. McCarthy. Your job is to sit here, no matter how long it may take, and deliver correct justice!" Diamond drove home.

Eyes were wide and breath was held as Diamond's astonishing speech abruptly ended. Even Victoria Stockford was amazed at the way Diamond had flipped Linda's own speech against her.

Just as Diamond began to walk away, she stopped and turned back to face the jury with the first smile any of them had seen all day. "Thank you for your time and cooperation," she added while removing her glasses and catching eye contact with the thirteenth juror, who was smiling back.

If it was anywhere else but a courtroom, applause would've erupted with a roar. But it wasn't. Everyone remained silent as the first witness was called to the stand and sworn in to tell the whole truth, and nothing but the truth.

Chapter 38

The next morning, Starr woke up and jumped down from the top bunk. She wanted to get an early start on the eventful two days she had been planning. She looked down at Kathy, who was still sleeping peacefully.

"Rise and shine, sleepyhead," Starr yelled as she mushed Kathy's head.

Kathy woke up not alert. It took a few seconds for her whereabouts to register. She looked up and found her newfound idol smiling down at her. She smiled back, sat up, and curled her legs into an Indian-style sitting position. "I dreamed I was home," she stated while wiping her eyes as she yawned.

"Everywhere is home if you're alive. Never forget that." Starr dropped a jewel on her. "Now, c'mon, let's wash up and go get some breakfast. I got a surprise for you."

"Really?" Kathy asked with animated excitement.

"Yup, and you're not the only one."

Kathy didn't know exactly what that meant.

After breakfast that was prepared by one of the Double Gs, Dominique came and got Kathy from Starr. She brought her to her room and sat her on the desk stool. She looked down on her, smiling, with a pair of scissors in her hand. "Now, let's see what we can do with you."

Everyone in the pod noticed that Starr was serious about protecting Kathy, so they stayed clear of her. But two people still boldly watched Kathy's every move with disgust.

Starr strolled over by the glass doors where the phones were. She was just about to call Monica to see how things were going; then she abruptly hung up in the midst of dialing the number. She had caught eye contact with two more Double Gs who were on the other side of the pod. She flagged them over to the glass.

When they were done, Starr felt even more relaxed. She strolled back over to the phone and finished making her call.

Kathy watched with horror as her long fire-engine red hair fell to the floor. She wondered how Starr's friend had gotten such a large metal pair of scissors in the first place. She closed her eyes and just waited for it all to be over, especially the secondhand cigarette smoke.

Dominique was just finishing up when Starr burst into the cell grinning from ear to ear. "Wow, she looks great. I'll go next. I got a visitor coming."

Kathy brushed the excess hair off of her lap as she stood up. Dominique was holding a mirror facing her as she waved the flowing cigarette smoke away before she looked into it. After the initial shock set in, Kathy was pleased with her new look. Her hair was cut in a mushroom slant that fit her small face perfectly. She reached up and hugged Dominique.

"Okay, sit back down and let me do your makeup. I'll get you next, Starr. I'm in my white girl flow right now."

Starr laughed. She was about to sit on Dominique's bed and read the newspaper, until she looked out of the small window of the door and saw CO Williams creeping across the tier on the other side. He was sneaking into another girl's cell.

"Girl, what's up with this CO?" Starr couldn't help but ask.

"Humph. He be on some real freaky shit," Dominique wasted no time answering. "I heard they had to take him off the night shift because he was waking up in bitches' beds and shit. He even tried to hit on me when I first came through. I told that punta I like what he like." Dominique laughed as she took a quick trip down memory lane. "He ain't shit, girl. Fuck 'im. Long as he stay out of our way, that's his business," she ended.

"True," Starr agreed. "I just don't like him. I hate men, especially ones of his caliber," Starr expressed.

Kathy giggled, but stopped abruptly when Starr turned in her direction. Dominique put the finishing touches on her. Starr sat on Dominique's bed.

"Everything set?" she asked Dominique.

"Everything's a go."

Starr nodded. "Make sure stories are airtight. Yours included. I got this end covered."

"On it," Dominique replied.

Kathy sat there clueless, just listening to dialogue exchanged between her new friend and Dominique. She would soon find out, though. After a while, Kathy lost interest in what Dominique and Starr were talking about. Her thoughts soon drifted to her and Starr.

"Count time," was called. All of the female inmates hurried to their cells and were locked in. Two of them were happier than everyone else in the pod put together.

"You got it? Let me see," Erica anxiously spat as she hovered over Darlene's shoulder.

Darlene was sitting on the stool at the desk, folding a playing card in half. She then reached into the crotch area of her jumpsuit and dug deep into her panties to retrieve what she had longed for all day. She secretly left half of it stashed inside her vagina to keep for herself and only pulled out the first ball. She set it on the desk and cracked open the small balloon.

Every speck of it glittered like diamonds. The small rock was solid. *It's enough to last for the entire week,* thought Darlene. It was time for a taste test. Darlene chopped the ball up into the most pure powder form as possible. She then took her index finger, stuck the nail into the cocaine, and rubbed it across her gums. Erica did the same. They both got the stunning powerful effect from the freeze they were looking for. Their gums and tongues became completely numb. They both took turns sniffing lines that Darlene had separated for them. They were trying to achieve the maximum high the vision of the coke had promised them.

Darlene fed Erica first. She took the corner of another card, dipped the corner of it through the coke line, and held it under Erica's right nostril. Erica inhaled with a deep snort while holding her left nostril down. Her eyes almost popped out of her head as she stumbled backward after the hit.

"Whoa! That's that shit!" Erica exclaimed. She began to rapidly blink her eyes. The inside of her nose began dripping cocaine fluid down the back of her throat. The kickback was surreal.

Darlene couldn't wait for her turn. She took it upon herself to take heavy hits. The two began to devour the drug lines nonstop. Erica joined her in "Scarfacing" the lines. The high was kicking in much faster and stronger than any coke they had ever done before. Their brains began to pound inside their heads. They both began to panic. At the same time, they leaped up and stared into each other's faces.

"Your nose is dripping blood," Darlene informed Erica.

"Yours is too," Erica replied.

Both girls took their sleeves and wiped their nostrils. Bright red blood gushed out even more. They began to get dizzy. Standing up didn't feel like such a hot idea anymore. They both collapsed. Erica fell onto the bottom bunk. Darlene fell onto the floor in a failed attempt to reach for the sink. She rolled onto her back, out of breath, looking up at Erica, who was apparently suffering from a seizure.

Darlene watched as Erica's body went into convulsions and then just stopped moving altogether. Her eyes stared off into space. Darlene knew she was next. Her breathing started to work against her. Blood began to spill from her mouth as her last few thoughts provided insight into what was happening. She had just been murdered by her own greed. It was all a setup from the beginning and she had taken the bait and wouldn't live long enough to fight free from the hook. But she knew exactly whose line she had been caught slipping on. It all came back to haunt her.

That fuckin' bitch lured us in, Darlene concluded. Darlene couldn't believe she fell for the fifty-two fake out. She knew they knew she had connections and could get whatever she wanted when she wanted it. So instead of trying to extort Kathy, Starr's idea sounded a lot more appealing and profitable than hers once Starr and the rest of the Double Gs were released.

Starr had proposed she pay for Kathy's protection from them. It would save them the hassle of having to physically take the money from Kathy, and then wait for someone to smuggle in the drugs for them to buy; and they would be cheated twice by a smaller quantity of a low-grade quality. Starr had promised them a lot of the best. She even stroked their egos by making them feel like they were good candidates for being Double G members, but they would first have to prove themselves by falling back and showing patience. Starr vowed to deliver and she expressed that a woman in her position wouldn't compromise her word. That was Darlene's last thought before her young drug-addled brain froze up and shut down on her.

Chapter 39

Teya was a beautiful, bodacious gay sista in her late twenties, who was incarcerated for sex trading and human trafficking. She was accused of pimping underage girls across state lines. She was considered to be a certified street madam among other things. She would first turn young girls out herself and then coerce them into going out and working on the strip she practically ran. She brainwashed with the deception of love and loyalty until they were ready to kill for her if need be. She was turned in to the feds after the mother of one of the young girls tracked her down all the way from Texas to Las Vegas and informed the local police. The mother's call to the locals launched a sting operation that led to the feds coming in.

Now, here Teya was, on pod B. Although she usually stayed to herself on the streets, Teya had two fetishes: gentlemen clubs and big-boned women. Which was why it was an actual club where she had secretly fallen in love with Starrshima at first sight. Everything about Starr turned Teya on.

She knew what the Double Gs stood for, being a plus-sized woman herself, standing at the even height of six feet, with 260 pounds of sex appeal and hips and ass for days. To top it off, Teya had a face to die for, which made it easy for her to recruit other attractive women. She knew she was doing what Starr was doing, on a much smaller scale, which was why she jumped at the opportunity when it presented itself. She was a very laidback and quiet person, who always chose intellect over her emotions whenever making decisions. Rarely seen and never heard.

One of her other strong traits was studying people. She studied every one of the girls in the pod from the time she had stepped foot on the pod. It seemed to Teya that once Starr had come in and put her muscle down and it was revealed who she actually was, every chick who thought she was big and bad in the pod was competing for her approval, hoping to be recruited. It was apparent to Teya that none of them knew anything about what Starr really represented or what the Double Gs actually stood for. Teya knew exactly who Starr was, though, and she knew the power of her organization.

She knew she was a force to be reckoned with and the Double Gs were a group of thorough women in position. She learned all of this just by frequenting the Double Gs establishment. Teya often took her personal workers to Club Panties, where she would auction them off to the drunk, horny guys staggering out of Club Emerald. The business had been great from the very start and was currently still flowing under the command of her underling.

There was nothing like living under the same roof with Starr. Getting to watch her in her natural element was alluring. Teya got to witness, firsthand, that Starr was indeed the real deal. She was not only gangsta on the streets because she had a team, but she could hold her own behind the wall as well, Teya drew the conclusion. It heightened the level of respect she had for Starr and her organization that Teya so desperately wished to be a part of ever since she had discovered what they were about.

Teya may have been a quiet woman, but she was far from shy. She was more of a quiet storm. Whatever she wanted she went after with no reluctance. This was no different. She wanted to be a Double Gs member and the only thing that was standing in her way was air and opportunity. The point finally came where she felt she couldn't wait any longer.

She had made up her mind that, after count, she would make her way over to where Starr's cell was. Teya lightly knocked on the cell door. Starr and Kathy were engaged in conversation during the unexpected visit. Starr turned and saw Teya's beautiful face staring through the cell door window. Starr waved for her to enter. Teya stepped in.

"What can I help you with?" Starr asked with a straight face, sitting next to Kathy on the bottom bunk.

"Hi. I'm sorry to bother you. I know you don't know me, but I'm—"

"Teya," Starr finished her introduction. "Teya McCoy. You run a spot downtown off Freemont Avenue. What can I do you for?" Starr crossed her legs and interlocked her fingers of both hands together over her knees.

Teya was thrown back and surprised Starr knew who she was. The two of them had never so much as had a word or exchanged any looks on the streets or since she had been on the pod. It took a second for the initial shock to settle. "How did you know?" Teya managed to ask.

"It's my job to know. I know detailed information about everyone who attended my club more than twice," Starr stated. "So what's on your mind?" Starr reestablished the point that she was trying to skip the small talk. She already had an idea why Teya was there.

Starr had reached out to Monica and had her put ten grand into an account given to her by Dominique. Once the money reached its destination, Dominique informed her about the setup and agreement she and another female inmate had. That agreement was with Teya. Starr knew Teya was Darlene and Erica's prison drug connect, which was why she was chosen. Teya was appointed the honor of masking the crushed-up glass mixed in with battery acid.

The sound of Starr's voice brought Teya back to the present. "Umm, well, this may sound strange, but I was kinda looking for a way in. I've always wanted to be a member, but I've never approached anyone." She stared into Starr's eyes. "This might not be the time right now, but it might be the only opportunity I get before I start my sentence," Teya revealed.

Starr studied Teya long and hard without saying a word. She knew all about Teya's private nighttime services. She also knew Teya was a leader, one who took care of her women, and Starr respected that. In fact, Starr had personally chosen the Freemont Avenue area for Felicia to carry out her first mission on Officer Blake. She trusted the environment that Teya had constructed on her own.

Teya had turned a dead back street into a personal empire. Starr noticed everything that Teya did came down to business being a number one priority. Starr knew Teya wanted to join their organization. She was actually on Starr's radar prior to Teya being arrested. When Dominique first told her who the drug connect was, Starr had already figured she could kill two birds with one stone, literally. Starr had already anticipated things going according to plan on Teya's end. It was the perfect initiation for Teya, thought Starr.

"Congratulations," Starr calmly announced. "You've been chosen for initiation to become one of us. We will get together later and I'll give you your instructions to carry out. If and when you succeed, I will have two members to witness you being sworn in. And, good job on that other thing. See you later," Starr ended abruptly.

Teya was speechless. She had no clue Starr had already had it in her plans to make her a member of the Double Gs. She stood there frozen for a second, as she watched Starr resume her conversation with Kathy. At that moment, in her mind, she vowed to ride with and for Starrshma Fields to the end of time.

Chapter 40

Throughout all the adversity, drama, and lack of the secret identity of Agent McCarthy's inside agent, Officer Douglass's testimony was still the key part of the entire investigation. Agent McCarthy's goal may have been to get Queen Fem, but Agent Reddick's only concern was bringing down Starrshma Fields and anyone else claiming to be a Double Gs member.

To Agent Reddick, Queen Fem was either just a mythical figure to hide behind, or an old, washed-up has-been. In his eyes, Starrshma Fields was the prize. She was Agent Reddick's main focus. He was taking this investigation and operation in a whole new direction. To him, Agent McCarthy's approach was too soft and passive. Agent Reddick's plan was to fight fire with fire.

He underestimated the Double Gs, though. He had no clue that going up against them was like bringing a book of matches to a forest fire.

Chapter 41

A sharp tap echoed through the cell door's glass window. It was 7:00 a.m. "Douglass! It's time! Let's go!" a guard's voice yelled at him.

Officer Douglass climbed out of his cell's bunk and strolled over to the sink's mirror. He fixed his tie. The agents had been kind enough to bring him an all-black dress suit. They felt it to be appropriate for the unfortunate occasion.

Officer Douglass's wife's voice haunted him in his mind as he stared into the dull mirror. He couldn't seem to get the voice on the phone out of his head. There was nothing left for him to do other than not let their deaths be in vain, he reasoned with himself. *I have to finish what I started,* he concluded. He planned to do everything within his power to send the Double Gs to hell. Even if he had to fabricate a few things to ensure their incarceration, he was willing to go the distance.

Officer Douglass was exactly what the feds needed. They knew he would be relentless with his revenge. The feds kept him in protective custody with around-the-clock security at his door; two agents rotated shifts at all times.

Agent Donahue and Detective Andrews were Officer Douglass's personal escorts to the funeral. Out of respect, they too were both dressed in all-black attire. Detective Andrews had been on the force about five years longer than Officer Douglass. The two of them had always shared a mutual level of respect for each other. That's why most of what was happening was still hard to believe for Detective Andrews. Watching Officer Blake and Agent Coulter die with his own eyes still haunted him. He only felt a little sympathy for Officer Douglass but had no words for him as they interacted.

Detective Andrews placed the ankle restraints around Officer Douglass's feet and handcuffed him in the front. He then folded the suit jacket over the cuffs to hide them. He knew how embarrassing it would be for him to be there having to face both sides of the family and the many others who would be in attendance. One thing was certain to them all: no matter whether the Double Gs killed Loretta and Cameron in retaliation, it all traced back to the evil that Officer Douglass had done. He was the one they would've all rather seen getting buried instead of his wife and daughter.

Officer Douglass was escorted outside of the detention center and ushered into a black Impala with tinted windows. Agent Donahue drove while Detective Andrews sat in the back next to Officer Douglass. Two U.S. marshals in a Ford Taurus led the way.

It was a twenty-minute drive. The beautiful day was bright without a cloud in sight. The Impala pulled up to the memorial and parked behind the long line of cars of the people who came to attend the funeral and burial services. People Officer Douglass recognized were scattered all over the field, walking through the vibrant green grass, greeting and consoling each other before they took their seats.

Due to procedural tactics, Agent Donahue got out of the vehicle first to scope the scene. The U.S. marshals had parked farther down, doing the same. The one who was driving the Ford Taurus gave Agent Donahue a long-distance head nod of approval before they both took their positions standing across the street from the funeral.

Detective Andrews exited the Impala, pulling Officer Douglass out along with him. Officer Douglass was nervous. The turnout was much larger than he expected. All eyes were on him. Breath was being gasped, hums of disappointment were being sung behind tight, locked lips, and negative whispers were exchanged.

He was almost ready to turn around, but he quickly caught sight of the open caskets up front. He then proceeded to walk closer until he could see them both. They were both lying peacefully. A white rose sat on the center of both their heads to cover up the tiny hole that was used to release their souls into the air.

There was a seat for him and his two escorts up front. The three of them passed the many rows of anger-filled family members sitting in their white folding chairs. Officer Douglass was glad to have everyone sitting behind him. Their eyes burned a hole in the back of his head as he sat down. But nothing else mattered other than what lay in front of him: a large casket, sitting beside a smaller one. Nothing could hold back his tears as the preacher approached the podium.

Chapter 42

At 5:30 a.m., Kathy found herself up again after a short sleep. She hadn't even gone to bed until 3:30. She was up thinking, horrified about the most recent events that had taken place. She started to question who she was, and who she was becoming. First, it started with her case. She had thrown her life away, and all for nothing. She went from being a straight A student, who was skipping grades because she excelled at a much faster rate than others her age, to a criminal indicted by the United States of America.

Next to haunt her mind was her cellmate Starr, who was undoubtedly her only reason for being comfortable or even surviving in jail in the first place.

"You need anything?" Starr offered Kathy on her way out.

Kathy didn't know what to think. This was the first time Starr spoke more than a word to her and she didn't know whether to take her on her offer or to reject it. She wasn't in the mood for games.

"I'm good," Kathy lied. She did want something from Starr but she hadn't decided whether Starr would deliver.

"Well, if you change your mind," Starr let out before she exited the room.

Kathy lay down. She wanted to tell Starr to stay and play. Kathy wanted to know if Starr could move her fingers at lightning speed, if her kisses were soft, what her nipples felt like. If she was up to the task of being Starr's bitch.

Fear of rejection kept her from voicing her need and, because of that, it would continue to go unmet. Kathy didn't want to say anything and find out that Starr didn't go for white girls. She wanted to be sure. After all, the two of them would have to live together and the last thing she needed was to be uncomfortable around her bunkmate.

A part of Kathy wanted to run to the door to see if she could steal a glimpse at Starr. And if she did, what was she going to do about it? It wasn't like Starr was looking back at her or had voiced any interest in her.

The thoughts left her mind and Kathy got in her bunk and got under the sheets. In her cell, she felt safe taking a nap while Starr was out handling her business. The pod was loud and she knew it would be a minute before she slept.

I want a radio so I can tune these other bitches out, Kathy confessed to herself. She wondered if Starr could get it for her, but she didn't want to owe extra favors or be indebted to the woman forever. And the last thing she wanted was an *Orange Is the New Black* experience. She caught a few episodes before she got locked up and she concluded that the television show, nor the book it was based on, would adequately prepare her for this experience. Kathy would have to live day by day and determine what prison life was going to be like for her.

Sleep invaded Kathy's mind and her eyelids felt heavy. Her world got dark and her body rested. Soon she saw a familiar purple light that beamed in the distance. Going toward the light, she found herself transported to her bedroom.

Plush chocolate-colored Cindy Crawford bedding covered her twin-sized bed. Her matching dark chocolate dresser and nightstand popped up from the eggshell white floor. The familiar smell of cinnamon and chamomile soothed her spirit and brought a sense a calm to her soul.

Kathy was home. No bullshit from work. No ailing parents to take care of. And no bad-ass kids who weren't hers to look after. It was just her.

Running water caught her attention and she wasn't sure what to think. Kathy just knew she was by herself.

"Baby, can you hand me a towel?"

Kathy looked around and couldn't identify the woman's voice that just called her "baby." The last time she was someone's "baby" she had a man who hit her in between hitting it. She knew it wasn't Jamarcus because that motherfucker was locked away in a mental institution. The PTSD became severe as Jamarcus couldn't separate his life in Afghanistan from the life they used to live together.

"Baby, you hear me?" the soft, feminine voice called out to her.

"Yeah, I'm coming," Kathy answered. She rushed to her closet and pulled out a set of purple towels. She had no idea who was in her bathroom, but she was determined to find out. Quickly, she glanced at the top of the closet to see if the 9 mm that Jamarcus had left behind was still in the small black box he kept it in.

"Kathy." The figure startled her. Upon closer inspection, she couldn't believe that Starr was standing in her bedroom buck-naked. She quickly shook her head because she didn't know she was a lesbian or that she had a girlfriend. "I was waiting on you."

"I'm sorry," Kathy offered. "I had a flashback of Jamarcus and—"

"Girl, what did I tell you about thinking about that sorry-ass nigga?" Starr questioned as she took the towels out of Kathy's hands.

Kathy couldn't remember what Starr said about that sorry-ass nigga. She couldn't even remember how Starr got in her bedroom or how, all of a sudden, she was "baby."

"*That nigga locked up and he can't get you.*" Starr wrapped her wet arms around Kathy's shoulders. She had turned the towel into a makeshift dress. The plastic shower cap protected what Kathy was sure was a perm underneath.

Being able to look Starr in the eyes and be face to face had Kathy feeling good. She leaned in for a kiss and was happy that Starr slipped her a nice, thick tongue.

"*Aww, Kat Kat, come on. I just got out of the shower.*"

Not only was she "baby," she had a nickname, "Kat Kat." This was something Kathy could get used to.

"*But I'm baby.*" Kathy looked down and knew she was fresh in the cream-colored mesh Baby Phat athletic suit. Kathy knew she hadn't done anything strenuous and she smelled her baby powder and Heat by Beyoncé fragrance.

Starr stepped back and unzipped the jacket. Kathy stepped out of her Timbs as she and Starr shared another kiss. Her nipples hardened and she loved the way they rubbed across Starr's. Kathy couldn't remember how her clothes came off so fast, but what she did like was that Starr was lying on top of her on the bed, kissing her, slurping her down like a decadent banana split.

The juicy clitoris facing Kathy encouraged her to reach up and pull Starr's ass down so she could put her lips on Starr's other lips. As her tongue flickered across Starr's mother-of-pearl, Kathy felt the same sensation as her legs opened. Starr's tongue licked and sucked on Kathy's clit while French kissing her thick pussy lips.

"*Aaaawwwhhh, baby.*" Kathy let out a moan as she happily returned the favor. She stuck her tongue as far into Starr as she could, stiffening her muscle in an attempt to stimulate the clit like a dick.

"*Yes,*" she heard Starr moan as her woman rode her face like a horse. The smell of her fresh pussy motivated

Kathy to move her head up and down, providing comfort for Starr's ride. Kathy snuck her right middle and index fingers to her mouth and sucked on them for a minute. Without warning, she slipped her saliva-lubed fingers in Starr's ass, tightening her grip, and she continued to lick for nectar in her human dessert.

Kathy whimpered as she felt Starr's fingers inching closer to her ass. She relaxed, taking comfort that Starr was being gentle and seeking invitation. Unlike Jamarcus, who rammed his thick, pulsating eight-inch dick inside her and often forgot that it wasn't a pussy, Starr made anal penetration fun.

The two continued tasting each other and penetrating one another, taking turns riding each other's faces and grinding wet pussy lips onto each other's mouths.

When Starr got on top, she slid off of Kathy and turned her body to where they were facing one another. She and Kathy shared an orgasmic kiss, each feeling the trembles in their bodies.

"Ahh," Starr exhaled as she kissed Kathy. Sneakily, she slipped her fingers between Kathy's folds as she took control of Kathy's right breast with her tongue. Moving it in circles, she traced the edges of her ribbed areola and, after taking three laps, she gently bit Kathy's nipple.

"Damn," Kathy cried as her waterfall escaped the dam that Starr was working fast to break. Her body quivered again as another waterfall released after having her right nipple attacked by Starr's tongue.

"Baby, I love you," she heard Starr whisper in her ear.

"I love you too."

"You love who?" Kathy's dream was interrupted by Starr and a few of her girls staring at her from the entry of their cell.

Kathy felt nervous because she had meant to take a nap, not fantasize about what it would be like to get fucked by her bunkmate. Her breathing was labored and she panicked as she looked at each of the women.

Oh, my God, what if she's not gay? Kathy feared for her life because she knew had heard that in some prisons lesbians were beat up by their straight roommates. *And what if Starr has a girlfriend already? Damn it, Kathy!*

"Girl, you got to learn to do that shit in the shower," one of the Double Gs members suggested. "All that ooing and ahhing, you ain't Whitney Houston. They lock bitches in the hole for shit like that."

"And your bed is wet, girl; clean that shit up," another Double Gs member commanded.

It was when Kathy sat up that she realized that it was her finger, not Starry's tongue or fingers, bringing her body to a frenzy.

Her fucking fingers.

To avoid trouble, Kathy quickly jumped out of bed and did as she was commanded. Kathy snatched the uncomfortable, soaked white sheets of the thin twin mattress.

"Y'all get out of here. I got this," Starr commanded and, just like that, the other women were out of the room.

"I'm so, so—" Kathy blurted out. She didn't want her ass whooped and, judging by the big girls who were following, not standing with Starr, Kathy knew she was in some shit.

"Girl, don't be sorry," Starr offered nonchalantly as she hopped on her bed. "Just next time, when I ask your ass if you need anything, that's the time when you open your mouth and say you need a release. And, girl, I'll give you all the time you need. Just don't have this place smelling like fish and shit."

Unconsciously Kathy inhaled and was thankful that her womanly fragrance did not permeate the room. "Thank you."

Kathy was pleased that she wasn't getting her ass beat and if a verbal reprimand was all Starr was going to give for getting off in their cell, she'd gladly take it. Kathy put her soiled sheets in her dirty clothes bag and quickly moved to put a clean set of sheets on the bed. The bell rang and she knew her recess time had come to an end.

As she made her bed and straightened up her side of the room she stole a quick look at Starr. Even in a prison jumpsuit and red Kool-Aid-dyed short finger waves, Starr was still the shit.

And Kathy was glad that she could get up and look at her every morning.

Then, there was her new appearance. She wasn't the young, innocent Katherine States, daddy's little angel, anymore. No. She now wore a short hairdo, and makeup, and a new bad attitude. That wasn't the half. Kathy had genuine love for Margaret. Sure, what Margaret did to her was wrong, she knew, but did she get what she deserved? Her thoughts were racing at a rapid pace. Was it worth it? Was the taste of revenge bitter, sweet, or both? Maybe. Maybe it was just one of those instances where no one would win. Did that make it right? Did it make them even? But what about the latest?

Last night. Those screams. The cries for help. Kathy rewound the memory in her head and watched as Yolanda walked into Darlene and Erica's cell and found them dead. The lifeless corpses were carried out on stretchers as the female inmates stood in their cell door windows and watched. They hadn't been let back out since.

Kathy peered up at Starr. *It had to be her work. Why was she so ruthless? Here she is sleeping peacefully, right above me, as if nothing happened. Should I be around her? She's a murderer. Am I safe? What if she ever mistook me as someone who would cross her?*

What does she even expect from me? What can I do for her? I'm just a young, inexperienced girl. Does she have a hidden agenda? Should I trust her? What if she—

Her thoughts were interrupted by the sudden sound of Starr's voice. "Hey, you. Whatcha doing up so early?" Starr asked after rolling off the top bunk. It was the first time they had spoken since the lockdown. They both had pretended to fall right asleep, but they were really wide awake, thinking. Starr was wondering if all she caused was worth it. In the end, she didn't regret it one bit.

"I couldn't sleep," Kathy answered. She felt bad knowing that Starr was just trying to protect her. She started to rationalize things by placing the blame on the victims.

Kathy instantly shook off her jitters and went back to following the most proven friend she ever had.

Aside from the speculative whispers, breakfast was pretty quiet. One thing was on every one of the girls' minds, and one thing only: the close proximity of murder. Each of the girls had been on the pod with Darlene and Erica for quite some time. Although they may not have condoned how the two drug addicts were doing their time, they never wished death on them. The faint stench of their corpses were still in the air.

Starr was suddenly viewed in a much different light now. Even though it was all just pure speculation, everyone chose to believe the only version of the story that was being driven. Starr got crossed and once again proved that she wasn't to be fucked with. Even while incarcerated.

After breakfast was over, Starr stood leaning over the top tier in front of her cell watching over everyone's movement. Most of the girls had gone back to their beds. A few of them sprinkled around the televisions sipping coffee, mostly the white ones who felt out of place during any later time of the day when everyone else was out and about.

The officers' shifts had changed. Starr watched CO Williams sway through the pod doors, hauling his knapsack over his shoulder, walking as if he owned the world. *Sometimes the world comes crashing down on you,* Starr thought as she ice-grilled CO Williams.

Chapter 43

Teya had been the first one out of her cell. The first thing that she did was go into the orderly closet and get the cleaning supplies. She scrubbed her cell down until it was spotless and then headed for a refreshing shower. When she got back to her cell she dolled herself up really nice. Her makeup was on point. She smelled great and she had on a snug, curve-hugging two-piece jumpsuit.

Next to Starr, she was the prettiest girl in the pod. Her hair was long and golden. Her complexion was creamy butterscotch. There wasn't a single scar on her body other than the scratches on her shoulders from fighting off two grown men who tried to kidnap and rape her when she was just twelve years old. The mental scars left proved to be much deeper. Her perky breasts were full of life. She perfected an enticing strut. Her bright, glossy lips made her succulent, inviting to all those who stared into the light red sprinkle of freckles on her face. Everything about Teya on the outside certified the stamp of beauty. But her mental didn't match up with the visual. Much like Starr, she could quickly end up being the coldest bitch you would've wished you never met.

CO Dylan Williams was a twenty-seven-year-old smooth dark brown brother with wavy jet-black hair. He was five feet eight inches, and 190 pounds. He was real cocky in a fake pretty-boy sort of way and he pretended to be tough. He always claimed how he was really from the streets and he was still in them but just hadn't gotten caught yet. He had been working as a CO for the past five years. His father, who also happened to be one of the captains there, had gotten him the job. Truth be told, they weren't from the streets at all. CO Dylan Williams had lived in the suburbs and attended private schools most of his life. He only broke out of his shell after finally being allowed to enroll in a public high school. That's when his good grades began to flip-flop and decline until becoming a CO was his only choice. Along with the government benefits, he took full advantage of the personal perks he felt came with the job.

He was never known for being much of a ladies' man. But it all changed once he started working in the women's pods A and B, where most of the female inmates were facing lengthy amounts of time going without sex with a man, so they worked with what was in front of them and CO Dylan Williams kept himself an option in front of them. He would smuggle in whatever it was they wanted and they would sexually express their gratitude. Most of the other guards knew what was going on but turned a blind eye to it, on the strength of the respect they had for his father. There was one specific woman CO Dylan Williams wanted to sample from the moment she stepped into the pod with her bedroll. He had originally shot his game, based on a false sense of security, at her every chance he got; but he was rejected each and every time.

Teya was never into men since her attempted rape occurred. CO Dylan Williams knew it. Those were the ones he went after the hardest. The challenge was gratifying. The newbie Starrshma Fields would've become his top pick, but he stayed up on current events and knew she wasn't to be tested. He decided to stay in his lane.

CO Dylan Williams dropped his bag into his desk chair and overlooked the pod. While standing there taking the last sip of his bottled water, something caught his peripheral vision's attention. He cut his eyes to the right and there she was looking sexier than ever before. He swore he could smell her from where she stood.

Teya was standing in her cell doorway, eyeing him down with a seductive gaze, as if he was the only one who could put out the fire in her panties. He tried hard to not look surprised as she curled her pointer finger at him, summoning his presence. He shot back the best smile he could produce and, as inconspicuously as he could, he looked behind him at the control bubble, knowing old Mr. Edmond was sleep. When he got to the door, Teya reached her arm out and gripped him by his uniform tie, pulling him into a strong, passionate tongue kiss as he shut the cell door behind them.

Although CO Dylan Williams knew they didn't have much time, he still had every intention of making it last. It was Teya who broke up the kiss. She seductively pushed him away from her body with sensual aggression and began a hypnotic exotic strip tease in front of him. Teya slowly removed her shirt and maneuvered her body the way she saw the women at the gentlemen's club do.

CO Dylan Williams hungrily licked his lips and took a quick step toward her. Teya pushed him backward until the backs of his knees folded after hitting the bed, flopping him into a sitting position. She stepped in between his legs and bent her right knee up to plant her bare foot in front of his groin. She ground her body to the rhythm of the nonexistent music that CO Dylan Williams swore he could hear as he watched her thunderous hips wind in a sensual motion. As much as he was enjoying the show, CO Dylan Williams felt it was time to be a part of it.

Teya could feel CO Dylan Williams's eyes glaring at her as she passed to get her lunch. She knew that he was up to something but she paid him no mind. Her focus was on getting her plate, finding out what was going on in the yard, and making her way back to her bunk. She got in and acted like the model inmate.

The minute she saw him lick his lips, she knew she had him. Truthfully, the thought crossed her mind to find out how those soup coolers would feel on her pulsating clit. At times, she thought about him and wanted the dick, mainly because she had never willingly had it and enjoyed it.

The plate of a hot dog and fries, and an artificial orange drink, were passed her way. Hiding the look of disgust, she put on a smile when she took her plate and then rushed to make her way to her seat. Teya wished she had her earphones and radio so she could tune out the other broads, but she needed to focus on the task at hand.

Finding a seat, Teya made her way to the unclaimed bench in the cafeteria. The other broads were nice today. She could see Starr watching in the distance and other members of the Double Gs spread out within a three-row vicinity.

I can't wait until I'm a Double G, she motivated herself as she kept her eye on CO Dylan Williams. The way he looked with his light brown eyes, it seemed as if they never left her ass. She put a subtle extra bounce in her step. Teya slightly glanced to her right side and could see that she had CO Williams's mind occupied.

I fucking hate hot dogs, Teya thought as she took a seat and opened the packet of ketchup and slowly thumbed the contents out of the packet and put it on the meat. With the mustard pack, she did the same and got pissed that they didn't offer relish. When Teya ate hot dogs, that was her favorite part.

When she looked to see where Starr was, the woman wasn't anywhere to be found. She noticed a couple of the

Double Gs missing as well. *Damn it, I wanted them to see this,* Teya pouted to herself. She looked around and found a few other broads caught up in their own stuff. That was fine with Teya.

CO Dylan Williams moved in position to get a closer look at Teya and she discretely made sure that none of the other COs who were looking and noticing that CO Dylan Williams was distracted.

Picking up the hot dog, Teya slowly brought the food to her mouth and she opened wide. She moved her lips slowly across the food until she got to the halfway point. The hot dog was pulled out a little bit then bitten. The look on CO Dylan Williams's face was of pure amazement. She knew that he wondered what it would be like to have his dick in her mouth.

As soon as Teya was confident that no one saw her inappropriate innuendo, she made a go for it again, this time putting the rest of the hot dog in her mouth and chewing on the food slowly. She moved the food from one side of her mouth to another, faking a sucking movement that could be seen from the side of her mouth. CO Dylan Williams's eyes were closed briefly before looking around and focusing on Teya.

The fries were eaten slowly. Teya licked her lips between each bite. Unlike the hot dog, Teya relished being able to show off more of her oral skills. Some of the fries were slowly sucked into her mouth before going down. A few of them she twirled with her tongue. As she saw the pleasure in CO Dylan Williams's eyes from watching her freak show with food, she took a slight pleasure in pretending she was doing all the thing to his dick. Having seen him erect, she knew CO Dylan Williams was working with big one; and, low key, she'd need all the practice she could get.

Once the fries were gone, she opened the carton of artificial orange drink and drank it like she was gulping down a Pepsi. Satisfied that her job was done, she gathered her trash, put it on the tray, and dumped her mess before walking the tray to the sink area and handing it to the inmate who worked the dishwashing section.

I hate that the Double Gs didn't see that shit. Teya acknowledged her disappointment as she headed outside to enjoy the rest of her rec time. She really didn't know what she wanted to do, but she knew that she needed to stay in CO Dylan Williams's sight at all times. Before she left the dining hall, she still didn't see a Double G in sight.

Outside, she saw some of her other friends sitting on the bench, looking over an old muscle magazine. That was as close to *Playgirl* as they were going to get.

"What you doing by yourself?" CO Dylan Williams broke her thought.

It worked. Teya praised herself. She was getting better at this seducing shit. "I'm working the yard to and fro, seeing who I can make friends with," Teya lied. That was the only one she could come up with at the moment.

"Shit, for a minute I thought you wanted to be my friend." CO Dylan Williams subtly palmed her ass. She looked around and saw that no one's eyes were on her.

"We can do that, depending on what kind of friend you want me to be," Teya offered as she led the way behind a building. CO Dylan Williams pulled her tightly to him and, as she faced him, she could feel his juicy lips on her neck. And his bulging member felt good as it slowly ground her midsection. Teya couldn't hide that she liked the way it felt. "You want to be that type of friend?"

"I'm not like this with everyone," his square ass replied.

Teya smiled to herself. The plan was working and she had CO Dylan Williams right where she wanted him. "Truth be told, I don't give a fu—"

"Don't curse," CO Dylan Williams warned her, reminding her that he was still in control.

"Just don't bring me nothing them other broads got is all I'm saying," Teya finished her thought.

CO Dylan Williams cupped her ass one good time before parting. "As often as we test y'all, you don't have to worry about me bringing no STDs or nothing like that to you." CO Dylan Williams departed as fast as he caught up with her.

Oh, my God, that dick felt good, Teya admitted to herself as she watched him walk away. She never told anyone, but she always had a fetish of watching a man's ass when he walked away. From the looks of it, CO Dylan Williams had the right amount of bounce to confirm he had enough to hold on to if she could get him on top of her.

Teya pretended she was crazy, dancing slowly to herself, enjoying the first touch from a man in quite some time. In the beginning, after the rape, it had been hard for her to even stand to be around a man or men, let alone be touched by one. But her eagerness to prove herself overpowered her fear of men. She had actually managed to become stronger after the ordeal and after her interest in the Double Gs.

From the looks of the yard, Teya knew she had a few minutes to get to the bathroom. As she made her way, she saw one of the Double Gs heading to the bathroom as well. She wondered if Starr was there, but she knew better than to seek her out. If Starr wanted to talk to her, she'd make herself more accessible.

Teya waited in line and, once a stall came available, she walked in and pulled her pants down. As she angled herself so she could aim and not hit the toilet, she noticed a small flip phone being slid under the stall.

The fuck? Teya wondered.

"Take it," she was instructed.

Following directions, Teya took the phone from her quickly, put it in her pocket, and got herself together to aim. She released, and was pleased that she didn't accidentally get any mess on her pants. As she finished, she felt the phone vibrate in her pocket. She dug it out and read the text message: Good job T. I C the mark is smitten by U. Don't get 2 comfortable w/the MFR because ur on a mission. Keep his dick hard & soon, you'll b where U need 2 b.

A hand stuck under the stall and Teya put the phone in it. Moments later, she left the stall and rushed to the sink to wash her hands. She looked around and couldn't see any of the Double Gs. She got some tissue to wipe her hands and disposed of them. She giggled at the thought of being invited to be one of his prison female harem and, until his usefulness was done, Teya had every intention of taking advantage to the fullest.

Teya closed her eyes, licked her glossy lips with her fully extended tongue, and stuck her left index finger into her moist mouth. She then pulled it free and stuck it into her panties while caressing her own breasts with her right hand. She rode her finger with the expression of ecstasy glowing all over her face. Her eyes stayed shut as she bit her bottom lip, moaning and sucking in air.

CO Dylan Williams decided not to be teased any longer. He stripped out of his shirt until he was fully bare-chested. He tried to stand up, but Teya kept his concentration on her. She leaned in and sucked his bottom lip with aggression then pushed him back down on the bed with both of her arms and sat on top of his waistline. She reached for his belt buckle and unfastened it along with his zipper. He arrogantly folded his arms behind his head, preparing to enjoy the ride. Teya slid his pants down to his ankles, and she began to massage his pipe staring up at her. Teya was performing her role well.

She stood up until the top of her head touched the upper bunk. She removed her own pants, but kept her panties on. Teya lowered her luscious thighs on top of CO Dylan Williams's and demanded that he suck her wet pussy through the thin cotton. CO Dylan Williams wasted no time replying with his tongue. He cupped both of her ass cheeks as she rode his face. He ignored the sound that came and went, too engrossed in the taste of Teya's instant climax through her panties and onto his lapping tongue. It wasn't the stimulation that CO Dylan Williams provided that caused Teya to cum; it was from watching the three girls who silently entered the cell unnoticed. She was showing off for them and the thought of what was going to happen next turned her on even more.

Teya just suddenly got up off of CO Dylan Williams's face. That's when he was able to get a surprisingly clear view of Dominique, who was holding a toilet plunger in her hand with one of the most insane smiles you've ever seen. He eyed the other two girls who were with her. One was holding a broom and the other was gripping a mop stick. CO Dylan Williams quickly panicked. He reached out for his clothes but they had been removed from the cell without him even knowing. He had no one to call for help. All in unison, all four girls jumped on CO Dylan Williams, straddling him.

Teya picked up the plunger, wondering if she should grease it up with her Vaseline. She sided against it. She was about to finally become an official Double Gs member and she wanted them to know just how hard she really went. Dominique pinned CO Williams's arms down while one of the Double Gs held his legs spread eagle and the other covered his mouth. CO Dylan Williams struggled to break free, but he was no match for the three burly women who had him subdued. Still, he fought with all his being, right up until the time the jolt of excruciating pain exploded within his entire body. Suddenly Teya wished that she had at least greased up the stick, but, oh the fuck well, it was what it was.

Chapter 44

Detective Andrews couldn't help but rub Officer Douglass's back in a futile attempt to console him as they sat and listened to the eulogy being delivered. Officer Douglass wanted to speak for himself at the funeral, but he wasn't allowed to. He was restricted to witness it and nothing more. They didn't want to provide too much exposure of his presence.

Everyone else sat there in tune with the program. The marshals stood across the street chain-smoking cigarettes and sipping cold coffee. Once in a while they scanned the perimeter.

Halfway into the ceremony, far up above in the sky the weirdest distraction presented itself. The preacher tried to ignore the annoying noise of an aircraft approaching. He paused and waited for it to pass. It never did. Instead, it hovered directly above, causing everyone to look up at the modern-style model. Right over them it began to perform stunts. It drew everyone's attention to the air. Even the marshals were looking up. They immediately began to spring into action.

"We gotta get that thing out of here," one marshal proposed. He reached for his walkie-talkie and requested to be dispatched to flight control.

Andrews, Douglass, and Donahue couldn't help but stare up at the interruption. It was evident it was a skywriter's plane. It started releasing bright white clouds of smoke into the cloudless sky. The smoke eventually began to form letters that turned into full words. Everyone stayed focused on the forming words that read, TIME FOR YOU TO JOIN THEM NOW.

Most were not familiar with what they believed to be some sort of advertisement and they drew their attention back to the minister.

Detective Andrews began to read the sentence aloud. Out of nowhere something smacked him in his face. The same happened to his partner. Both Detective Andrews and Agent Donahue used their hands to wipe their eyes clean from the unexpected fluid that splashed in their faces. Andrews was the first to clear his vision. He looked down at his hands. The reality of what had just happened instantly kicked in. No one had heard the muffled rifle shot, or seen the infrared beam spot itself between his eyebrows. No one witnessed the promised assassination actually happen as he sat between two of the most decorated law enforcement officers in the city. Not one person noticed until it was too late. Officer Douglass's head was already slumped backward. A panic erupted.

"Holy shit! Man down! I repeat, man down!" Agent Donahue yelled into his cufflink microphone as everyone at the funeral dropped to the grass and crawled around. No one knew where the shot came from.

Detective Andrews drew his weapon and aimed at the departing plane. He then swayed it back and forth around the vast area of the burial field. He wiped the remainder of the blood and brain matter from his face as he scanned the fleeting crowd. The marshals had seen the catastrophe from afar and ordered that the plane be tracked and detained in search of answers. They couldn't believe the daring murder had occurred. The grounds were now covered with countless members of law enforcement agencies. But it would all be much too late. The hidden assassin was long gone and Jake Stolkoff's plane had served its purpose. Jake Stolkoff showed up and did what he was paid to do. Unbeknownst to him, he was the key piece to the plan Starr had passed to Monica. He was exactly what he was supposed to be: a diversion.

Chapter 45

Felicia exited the bathroom of her double-level, three-bedroom home, drying her hair after the hot, long, steamy shower she had just taken. It had been a crazy week for her. Between keeping an eye on Monica for Diamond and staying on her own toes, with all that had been going on, she had been on constant edge. She still hadn't decoded the text she had received about not trusting anyone. She had fought hard to gain the position she was in and she told herself she would do whatever it took to keep it. Felicia had sacrificed her entire life as she once knew it to be a part of what she was. She had been with the Double Gs organization for years and had taken advantage of her position throughout them, without any harm done to her or backlash.

Now here it was: she was told to trust no one. Felicia was experienced enough to know she needed to get to the bottom of what the text message had meant. It would be the only way she could feel at ease again, she believed. Felicia removed the towel from her head. Her eyes grew cold by the uninvited guest who sat on top of her bed.

Clips figured it was either now or never. He felt he had gathered up enough information to present to the woman he had become infatuated with. He felt no shame for breaking into and entering her home. He would have rung the doorbell but sided against the idea, believing he would not receive a warm welcome. Judging by Felicia's facial expression, he concluded that he was correct.

Clips couldn't keep his eyes off of Felicia. He looked her up and down with lustful eyes. When she first entered the room dripping like chocolate, Clips's dick stood at attention. He licked his lips at the thought of what he would do to all of that thick, shapely flesh Felicia possessed.

Their eyes met for the first time. If looks could kill, Clips believed he'd be a dead man, just as he knew if she had access to one of the many guns he found stashed throughout the house he'd also be dead.

"Hello, beautiful," Clips spoke in the coolest tone he could conjure up. Despite the fact that he had a gun pointed at her, for some reason he felt a little nervous now that Felicia actually stood before him.

Felicia kept her eyes on Clips as she wrapped the towel around her body from the chest down. "Li'l nigga, you got less than half a second to rise up and get the fuck outta here before I change my mind," Felicia stated in an authoritative manner.

Clips let out a loud chuckle. "I don't think that's what you really want me to do." Clips spoke with confidence. Something in his tone alarmed Felicia.

She thought hard and quick. *What the fuck is that supposed to mean? What the hell does he think he know?* she pondered. The only thing she knew of Clips was that he was young, one of Prime's soldiers, and that he had a thing for her.

Clips cut her thoughts short. "I'm sure you're wondering why I'm here in the first place." A smirk appeared across Clips's face. "I know something about you that you'd wish I didn't." Clips let his words sink in before he continued. He could tell Felicia was processing them.

Felicia stared at him oddly. *Is this who I was being warned about?* Felicia wondered.

"I don't think your girl Starr would be pleased to hear what I have to say and like what I'd show her if I went to see her up in that county jail," Clips added.

If she wasn't sure before, she was now. Clips knew more than he should. Felicia cursed herself for coming out of the bathroom with her face covered, thinking about the .380 she had stashed up under her bedroom's bathroom sink.

At that moment, shit just got real for her. She knew she couldn't let Clips leave up out of her house. Her life now depended on it. Her thoughts did a hundred-yard dash. She knew she had to think of something quick to buy her some time. There was only one way to do that. There was no way she was going to let some young street punk put the press or outsmart her. She had come too far for this to be the final outcome.

"How much?" Felicia asked with attitude.

Clips laughed. "How much what?" he retorted.

"How much to keep your fuckin' mouth shut?" Felicia spat in disgust.

Clips began to shake his head slowly. He was becoming aroused by his own thoughts. *This shit couldn't have worked out any better,* he excitedly told himself.

"What I want, for starters, money can't buy," he replied devilishly. "Or, maybe it can." He flashed a grin that turned Felicia's stomach.

She read beyond Clips's perverted metaphor. *This piece of shit.* She gritted her teeth through clenched jaws. She knew she had to make a decision and fast.

This was not the first time she had been in this type of position and had to do what had to be done for the cause. She could hear the voice in the back of her head, *whatever it takes!* echoing in her mind. Like all the other times, Felicia jumped into character.

She licked her lips and dropped her towel. "Well, maybe we can work something out." She stepped over the towel and moved in closer to Clips. Clips became even more excited. He knew she was only pretending, but he didn't care. He had fantasized about Felicia since the first day he laid eyes on her. He had vowed that day that he would get her, one way or another, one day. That day had finally come. Clips rose up off the bed. By now Felicia had a fistful of Clips's young, thick cock.

"Yeah," he cooed. "Maybe we can," he added. He clumsily mangled Felicia's breast with one hand and began to fondle her roughly with the other. His heart rate increased. He was turned all the way on by the tightness and wetness of Felicia's juicy box. Felicia rolled her eyes as she slid her hand inside his True Religion jeans. She couldn't tell whether he was inexperienced or simply anxious.

"Calm down, daddy." She went into character once again. "Slow down and enjoy it," she suggested as she stroked Clips's hardness.

Her words struck a nerve. "Shut the fuck up!" he exclaimed. All in one motion, he sidestepped, spun Felicia around, and pushed her onto the bed. He didn't like to be told what to do in the bedroom. With an impotence issue, Felicia made him conscious of his insecurity. The only thing that could actually keep him aroused and turned him on was when he was manhandling a female. Felicia turned back to look at him.

"Turn the fuck around!" Clips ordered. He jerked his jeans down to his thighs.

Just get it over with, Felicia wished.

Clips massaged his semi-erect male member. He could feel it growing within his hand. He wasted no time ramming every inch of his rock-hard dick inside of Felicia.

"Goddamn!" he bellowed as he grabbed hold of Felicia's massive hips. You could hear the sound of his thighs smacking up against Felicia's voluptuous ass cheeks.

Clips lifted Felicia's cheeks. He held them up and spread them as wide as he could as he pounded away at her inner walls vigorously. Clips bit down on his bottom lip as he watched Felicia's cream coat his dick and he listened to her pussy talk. His thrusts became even harder by the sight.

"Yeah, you ain't no dyke. You lovin' this dick!" Clips boasted. He then took his thumb and forcefully pressed it inside of Felicia's brown eye. He held his thumb still while he long stroked her.

Felicia's body was shaking uncontrollably. It had been a long time since she had been penetrated and her muscles were having spasms from the foreign sexual acts. Although Clips was causing her body to have multiples, she was not enjoying it one bit. She had never been raped before, but she knew Clips's behavior warranted the title. Felicia's thoughts were immediately interrupted by the excruciating pain that came out of nowhere.

Clips pulled out of Felicia and, without warning, popped the head of his dick inside Felicia's asshole. Felicia closed her eyes to fight back the tears. Clips was now power-drilling her anus nonstop. Felicia just lay there and took the abuse. She could feel Clips's sweat dripping on her back as he rode her ass. It seemed like it would never end. Clips's pumps increased. Felicia could feel him tearing her insides apart. Three thrusts later, Clips hopped up.

"Agh!" he let out as he sprayed Felicia's ass cheeks with his thick, young juices.

Felicia couldn't fight the tears back any longer. Her butthole was sore and she felt like she had to use the bathroom. She lay on the bed feeling defeated. She had never endured what Clips had just put her through. Her emotions were in overdrive. She rolled over into a fetus position on her bed. She couldn't believe she had just been the victim of not only blackmail, but a rape.

She tried to collect her thoughts as she watched Clips waddle, with jeans still down to his thighs, and wipe himself off with the towel she had just dried off with. She couldn't help but notice the gun he had stuck in between his belt and his pants. The sight of it triggered Felicia's survival skills switch. It was evident Clips had searched her place from top to bottom, but there was one place she knew he most likely overlooked.

Felicia glanced over at the classical replica of the painting from the hit TV series *Good Times*. It was a long shot, but it was better than no shot at all, thought Felicia. She drew her attention back to Clips, who was in the process of pulling up his jeans. Felicia took a deep breath, then made a mad dash over to the wall painting. She wasted no time moving the painting to the side, revealing the wall safe she always kept unlocked.

"What the fuck!" Clips spun around and yelled. He was just finishing up fastening his Gucci belt when he detected movement from behind him. Clips instinctively reached for his hammer. By the time he drew it, imminent danger had already introduced itself to him.

The first shot Felicia let off tore into the flesh of Clips's collarbone, forcing his gun out of his hand. The impact was enough to send him to the floor. The second one grazed him on the side of the neck.

Clips screamed out in agony. A gust of confidence poured into Felicia. She knew what she had to do. She was in too deep and there was no turning back now. She knew if she didn't kill Clips, once he reported to Prime they would not only kill her, but blow everything she had worked so hard to build. Felicia made her way over to where Clips lay with the look of death plastered across his face.

"Do what you gonna do, you fat dyke bitch!" he spat.

Felicia was unfazed by his words. She cocked her gun and aimed it at his head, but she never got to pull the trigger. The shot came from out of nowhere, sending her flying across the room.

Clips looked over to his right where the explosion had come from. He smiled proudly. "My nigga!" he exclaimed.

Felicia looked up just in time to see Smoke emerge from the connecting room.

"Get yo' ass up," Smoke commanded Clips. He wasn't feeling Clips after watching him rape Felicia. The only reason he came to Clips's rescue was because he knew he wouldn't have been able to convince Prime that he couldn't prevent it. He had his twin cannons pointed directly at Felicia in case she tried to make a move.

"You know we gonna have to kill this bitch now, right?" Smoke said to Clips, who had managed to get up off the floor.

"It's whatever, yo," Clips barked. "All this bitch had to do was play by the rules," he added.

Smoke laughed. "Whose rules, homeboy? Where they do that at?" he asked, referring to the rape he had witnessed.

An embarrassed Clips immediately changed the subject. "Fuck all that!" he chimed. "I got this shit." Clips cocked his gun. Felicia closed her eyes.

"Stupid bitch!" Clips bellowed. He cracked Felicia on the side of her head with the butt of his pistol. The blow opened up a deep gash on the side of Felicia's face. She could feel the blood oozing out. She couldn't believe this was what it had come down to. Her throat became dry and the room seemed to be spinning.

"Fuck you!" she screamed out. "Double Gs for life!" she then chimed. The words came from out of nowhere. For some reason, the words gave her a boost of confidence. "Double Gs for life!" she repeated.

"Oh, yeah, Double Gs for life, huh?" Clips mocked. "No, bitch. Clips took your life!" he remixed, right before the door burst open and gunfire erupted.

To Be Continued